T0267882

PRETTY
FURIOUS

PRETTY FURIOUS

E. K. JOHNSTON

DUTTON BOOKS

DUTTON BOOKS

An imprint of Penguin Random House LLC, New York

First published in the United States of America by Dutton Books,
an imprint of Penguin Random House LLC, 2024

Copyright © 2024 by E. K. Johnston

Visit us online at PenguinRandomHouse.com.

Library of Congress Cataloging-in-Publication Data is available.

ISBN 9781984816139
1st Printing

Printed in the United States of America

LSCH
Design by Anna Booth
Text set in Sabon LT Pro

To Colleen, Erin, Krista, Leanne,
Sandra, Sarah, and Siobhan.

Obviously.

"I suddenly remembered my Charlemagne: Let my armies be the rocks and the trees and the birds in the sky."

—Dr. Henry Jones Sr.

CHARACTERS

THE CARTER FAMILY
Maddie Carter (June 11)
Janice Carter, mother
Peter Carter, father
Emily Carter, older sister

THE SHARPE FAMILY
Mags Sharpe (November 14)
Mary Sharpe (née Shropshall), mother
Theo Sharpe, father
David Sharpe, younger brother
Colin Sharpe, younger brother
Elsie Sharpe, younger sister
Clara Sharpe, younger sister
Frederick (Teddy) Sharpe, younger brother
Father David Shropshall, uncle
David Shropshall Sr., grandfather
Magdalen Shropshall, grandmother

THE JANTZI FAMILY
Louise Jantzi (January 27)
Julie Jantzi, mother
Hugh Jantzi, father
Aaron Jantzi, older brother
Paul Jantzi, younger brother

THE HOERNIG FAMILY
Jenny Hoernig (August 25)
Julia Hoernig, mother
Adah Hoernig, younger sibling
Char Hoernig, younger sibling
Dottie Hoernig, younger sibling

THE DALRYMPLE FAMILY
Jen Dalrymple (May 1)
Lisa Dalrymple, mother
John Dalrymple, father

OTHERS
Amelia Chaser, older local girl
Isobel Johnson, volleyball player
Elizabeth Stewart, grade 11 student (Mags's second cousin)
Dahlia Hastings, grade 12 student (Jen has a crush on her)
Peter Hastings, Dahlia's grandfather (David Sr.'s roommate)
Zac Hastings, Dahlia's brother
Constable Jake Postma, local cop
Reverend Alden, local Anglican minister
Adam Pedersen, local asshole
Margaret and Jan Pedersen, his parents
Davy MacGregor, a boy from Mags's church
Alice MacGregor, a competitive swimmer
Trevor Harrow, a boy from school
Elyse Ritsma, Isobel's cousin
Emily Postma, Jake's younger sister
Mr. Harrow, principal and later superintendent
Mrs. Fiske, current principal
Mrs. Heskie, music/French teacher
Mrs. Kelly, guidance counsellor
Mr. Kelly, phys ed/algebra teacher
Mr. Rogman, science teacher
Mrs. Miller, drafting/geography teacher
Mrs. Bowles, English teacher
Mr. Attis, history teacher
Mr. Carmichael, phys ed teacher
Mr. Kreskin, janitor

PRETTY FURIOUS

It occurred to me, at that exact moment, that I didn't know very much about bird watching.

"It's usually just called birding, Maddie," Constable Postma said.

He was standing well back from my car, the very picture of nonthreatening. Except that we were in the middle of nowhere, and he'd pulled up to ask what I was doing. He did not suspect that I was in the middle of a stakeout, because why would I be doing something like that?

"Whatever," I said. I held up my binoculars so he could see them. "I'm learning. I just want to be alone."

"Can't you be alone in your room like a normal kid?" he asked. It took him about two seconds to visibly regret his word choice.

"No," I said.

"Is everything okay at home, Maddie?" he asked. His tone didn't change, but he shifted slightly, entirely becoming the sort of cop people naturally fear instead of the affably concerned neighbour he usually tried to project.

"Sometimes I just want to be alone." I went easy on him. He'd had a rough few weeks, and it was my fault. Not that he knew that part.

"I understand," he said. "That's why I took up birding."

I glared at him, but he was trying to be "accessible to the community," so his laugh wasn't too scornful. He walked over to his squad car, and I watched him closely as he rummaged through the glove compartment. After a moment, he came back towards me carrying something. It was a little book.

Birds of Ontario.

"As long as it keeps you out of trouble," he said, passing me the guide.

I thanked him because that's how girls are supposed to talk to cops. Then he got in his car and crunched away through the gravel lot, leaving me alone again.

I held my binoculars in one hand and the book in the other, and then threw them both onto the passenger seat. I went back to looking across the bean field, listening to the wind as it rustled through the browning leaves.

Trouble was exactly what I was looking for.

Sixth Wish
(TWO MONTHS EARLIER)

It hadn't been anyone's business but hers that Amelia Chaser was pregnant, but in a town like Eganston, that didn't matter very much. The same neighbourliness that saw ladies in the grocery store ask about her health had them clicking her tongues the moment she was out of earshot, cooing about how they didn't like "all these new people" in town, like property values were the only thing that mattered. "You're such a good girl, Maddie Carter," they'd say, making it clear that it was a precarious scale that only slid one way. I hated it.

Amelia Chaser, to her credit, didn't fucking care. She wasn't going to be a farmer's wife—or a mother—at eighteen. She sat through a patronizing guidance counsellor appointment about her new university plans given her "developing circumstances," and was confessed by Father Shropshall, who apparently forgot that it takes two to tango. Then she got in the car with her sister, drove to London, and had an abortion. The next Sunday, Adam Pedersen, who wasn't going to be a father after all, was given Communion, like nothing had changed. Amelia made Father Shropshall deny her to her face. I was very proud of her.

It's not that Amelia and I were close. We'd never attended the same school, because she was Catholic, and she was older than I was. We'd overlapped in Girl Guides and curling, but not enough to know each other by more than small-town proximity. Amelia's rebellion happened to coincide with the moment I realized other girls—different girls—were people and not the enemy, and I was angry about how all the people who we were supposed to trust had betrayed her. I was angry that I might have betrayed her, too, if it had taken me longer to wake up.

The billboard went up a year later, the Monday before my eighteenth birthday, and it had festered in me all week. The Pedersens had fifty acres, most of it cleared for farming, and chose to set the sign up so that it faced the Chaser farmhouse. They weren't subtle. After two days of tractors getting stuck in the late spring mud, their revenge for Amelia killing their grandcells was revealed:

Abortion Stops A Beating Heart.

It was stupid, and it was pointlessly cruel. And it was all I could think about.

The Sunday after the sign went up, two of the five of us were parked by the cenotaph, engine off and the windows down. We were waiting for Mags Sharpe, whose parents were Catholic enough that they went to church every week, but not so much that they wanted to send their kids to a school system whose funding had been sanctioned by the UN. Mags had been in youth group with Amelia, and she was our primary source for information that hadn't been three steps through the rumour mill. When she slid into Jen Dalrymple's back seat, Mags was positively *humming* with emotion. It was the first time Amelia had been back in town since she left for school last fall.

"At least she got to go away for university," Jen said when Mags was done bringing us up to speed. Father Shropshall had actually tried to give her Communion this time, but she'd refused him. Jen's mum's car made alarming noises when it crossed 100 kph, so we couldn't speed that much. When we were out of town, she put it in cruise as a preventative measure. "It sucks how quickly the boy next door becomes the asshole who ruined your life."

"I think she's doing fine," Mags said. "I couldn't see her face when she refused my uncle, but Davy MacGregor was the altar boy this week, so he could see her face, and he looked like he was going to piss himself."

Davy played broomball at the provincial level.

"I just hate how everyone talks about it," Jen said. She slowed to make the turn off the highway and onto the sideroad. "Like it's all her fault she's—"

Unfixable. Irredeemable. Untouchable. Take your pick. At least Amelia was past the sugar stage, and was well into the spice of not giving a shit.

"Let's not talk about it," Mags said. She leaned on the car door, the wind whipping strands out of her French braid. "It's Maddie's birthday. You only turn eighteen once."

I didn't correct her by pointing out that my birthday had been last Friday, or that I actually *did* want to talk about it. It was just the three of us in the car. What I wanted to talk about was going to need all five, and the others knew it. Mags wasn't the only one humming. We'd been working our way up to this for a while. The last year—and the previous four birthdays—had been a lot, but it hadn't been enough.

You have to fight to make it through life with four best friends. You can't all fit in the same car—though we could now that most of us could drive—unless we used Mags's family behemoth, and every time a teacher assigned partner work, you had to negotiate.

Our elementary school had only had about three dozen kids per grade, and our high school wasn't much bigger, but it was never a sure thing we'd end up in the same classes. Geography and time and money and interests will pull you apart, but somehow we'd made it to the beginning of June with the end of grade twelve in reach, and we were going strong. Maddie and Mags and Jen and Louise and Jenny (who would probably be a Jen by now, were it not for a snap decision made by our nursery school teacher).

We spent most of our time at Louise Jantzi's house. Her parents had sold their dairy quota instead of modernizing it when we were in grade eight, on the grounds that they didn't want to spend the rest of their lives with a cow deciding whether they could go on vacation. The farm and all its buildings had been converted into something of a mishmash that Hugh Jantzi *refused* to call a "hobby farm," and one of the conversions had resulted in a rumpus room that wasn't attached to the house. They rented it (and barn space, as necessary) to the local 4-H club. It was wired and heated, had a refrigerator, a TV, and comfy seats, and was well out of earshot of any adult. Mags's basement definitely had better bathrooms, but Mags's basement was also available to the horde of younger Sharpe siblings, so we only went there on special occasions.

Eganston was the centre of our network, where Jen and I lived, and where we all went to school. The other three lived ten minutes out of town in different directions, which was a challenge in an area that couldn't even dream about public transit. Most of us counted down the days until we passed our G1 exits and could drive without an adult, even if we'd have to share the car with everyone in the family. Eganston didn't even have a Tim's, much less a movie theatre, so just being able to drive was kind of a thing.

Jen made the final turn onto Louise's side road. The side roads had all been named when 911 came to the area, but most people over the age of thirty still referred to Louise's sideroad as "the third" instead of Old Mill Road. The mill had been gone for a century, which made it even sillier, but that's what happens when you have to name a bunch of roads at once.

There were only two houses on Old Mill Road, and the Jantzis owned both of them. The first was barely livable. Louise's older brother had been slowly flipping it, but he'd gone off to Ridgetown last fall for the agriculture program, and work had slowed. The second, a sprawling three-storey red Victorian, was where the family actually lived.

Jenny Hoernig was waiting for us on the steps, and ran up once Jen had parked the car.

"Louise says that Maddie needs to stay in the car and count to one hundred before she comes up," she said, grinning. "And Louise needs you two to carry things."

Louise took birthday cake very seriously, and I knew that this cake in particular would be important to her. It wasn't because it was me, exactly, but this birthday represented something. I took off my seatbelt but stayed in the front seat. I put my hands over my eyes and started counting down, because it was a countdown sort of situation. I felt safe with my friends. I felt ready.

I walked into the barn, currently empty because lambing season was over, and went to the bottom of the ladder.

"Ready or not, here I come!" I said, stepping onto the bottom rung.

"Wait!" said Louise, right on cue. "You have to tell us what you want for your birthday wish!"

I took a deep breath, inhaling the multitude of smells that made a working farm: sheep, hay, shit, rust, gasoline. We'd grown up here. This town had made us. And it deserved everything that we gave back.

"My name is Maddie Carter, and I am eighteen," I declared. "And for my birthday, I want you guys to help me start a fire."

FIRST WISH

Property Damage

(OR: MADDIE'S 17TH BIRTHDAY)

1.

Maddie Carter

All the good stories are full of unfortunate wishes. Wishers who were clever enough to avoid all the rules-lawyering face off against wish granters who do their level best to exploit every possible loophole. It's magic and mayhem, and depending on whether it's a straight telling of the story or a deconstruction thereof, by the end of it, everyone has learned a lesson: wishes are dangerous.

And yet we wish. On stars, blasting through space. On coins, flipped into burbling water in the mall atrium. On loose eyelashes, which really grosses me out. And, once a year, on birthday candles.

This particular birthday, I turned seventeen. It wasn't a very important number. Two years until I could drink, one year until I could vote, and one year past getting my beginner's license. I didn't even really have a party. Mum and Dad had dragged us all out of bed at seven in the morning on Thursday so that I could open presents, and there had been a cake in the evening, but the bulk of the festivities had been shunted off to the weekend.

Mags must have called the moment she got out of church, because it was barely 10:30 on Sunday morning when my cell rumbled in my pocket. I was finishing my waffles, which dad only made on special occasions because they took forever. Even on vibrate, the noise was enough for my parents to hear. They pretended not to notice, but I knew they were dying for information as much as I was. The Catholic church in town had decent attendance rates, but this week was like an evil Easter: everyone turning out to see the mess.

My sister, Emily, did not pretend. She'd missed most of the action already, having been away at school, but she'd come home at the beginning of May in time for the main disaster, and she wasn't about to let post-birthday decorum block the gossip.

"Well," she said. "Answer the damn phone."

Neither of my parents could complain about her language, as that was what they inevitably—and affectionately—ended up yelling at each other every time one of their cells rang.

I shoveled the last bite of waffle into my mouth and slid off of my chair. I was out the back door and on the deck before any of them could shout at me, Emily's protest cut short by sliding glass. She'd find out. Where we lived, everyone always found out.

I flicked the answer button, and had barely scraped together a hello when Mags began talking.

"He did it, Maddie!" She was yelling in the quiet way you learn to yell when you have five younger siblings and parents who actually care about taking care of them. "My fucking uncle." Her voice was garbled. I could hear the murmur of people on the other end. No one yelled at her about language, but I figured everyone at St. Brigid's this morning had enough scandal to keep them happy. "Yikes," she said, and I waited impatiently for her to provide context. "Mum's yelling at him now. This is probably the end of family dinner for a while."

"Jesus, can you just come over?" I asked. "I can't keep Emily off of you, but Mum and Dad will respect a closed door. Probably."

"Are there any waffles left?" Mags asked. She was nobody's fool.

"There will be if you hurry," I told her. Emily was waving at me through the glass, demanding that I get on with it.

"I'm on my way," Mags said.

Every other person in our grade had gone to the MTO on the day of their sixteenth birthday to get their beginner's license and then immediately scheduled their driving test for twelve months later. If you took driver's ed, you only had to wait nine months (and your insurance was cheaper), so I had been able to drive by myself for three whole months. Mags on the other hand was in absolutely no hurry to become her family's third driver. What meant freedom for many of us would have meant chauffeur duties for her. She had her G1, so she could drive with a licensed adult in the car, but she kept putting off scheduling her exit test. As such, she would have to walk the four blocks between St. Brigid's and my house. There were waffles on the line, though, so it only took her a few minutes.

Mum had already added another plate to the table by the time I got inside, and Dad was coaxing the last few waffles out of the waffle maker and onto the warming tray. Emily, who hadn't spent more than the minimum required time at the table since she'd come home for the summer, took her seat. I drew lines in the remnant maple syrup with my fork.

"Remember, this is Mags's family," Mum said—not that any of us needed reminding that the parish priest was also her mother's brother. A knock sounded on the door, followed by Mags coming in and kicking off her shoes.

Emily was politely subdued by the time Mags made it to the kitchen, and I poured her an orange juice as Dad set the last two waffles on her plate.

"Thanks, Mr. Carter," Mags said. She waited for the same brief pause she always did when she ate with a family that didn't say grace, and then she tucked in.

"Was it really bad?" Emily blurted. She and Amelia were the same age, even if they hadn't gone to school together.

"It was kind of quiet," Mags said thoughtfully, after she swallowed. She cut up her next few bites, neat squares with syrup running down the corners. "All four Chases were there, and my uncle just walked past them."

"It didn't sound quiet when you called," I said.

"That's because I called you after Father Shropshall invited us all outside for the dedication of the memorial." Mags managed to say her uncle's title without hissing, but only just. She shook her head, and a few more strands of dark hair worked their way out of her braid. She probably ran the whole way here, ballet flats and all. "The Chases walked right to the parking lot, and about a third of the congregation went with them. Mum started yelling at Uncle David the moment he came outside. I left before she was finished, so I didn't get to see the damn thing."

My mother, who had resented Catholic Communion ever since my aunt had been excluded from it during a "nondenominational" retreat for cancer patients hosted by the Catholic Women's League, made a noise that sounded almost like a growl.

"That fucking thing," said Emily.

It was an unfortunate coincidence that the stone St. Brigid's had been planning to erect "in memory of the unborn" coincided with Amelia Chase's personal life, but even without an immediate example, I still hated it.

"That is exactly what my mother said," Mags said proudly. "Right in front of half the congregation and a visiting bishop, at the top of her lungs."

She deflated a little bit as she kept eating. Mags always put a brave face on things. She'd been brought up to—first to behave, second to set a good example, and now because it was a habit. She was starting to push back, though, and now her discomfort and dissatisfaction with life in general was showing through the cracks.

"I'm sorry, Mags," I said. I would have squeezed her hand, but I don't get between Mags and waffles. "It sucks that you're in the middle of this, along with everyone else."

"Are you girls heading to Louise's?" Mum asked, signaling that the discussion was over. For the table, at least.

"That depends on when I get the car," I said, sweet as maple syrup.

Emily had to drive to work, and my parents didn't like being left at home with no transportation. It had been awkward at the beginning of May, getting used to Emily being back just after I'd gotten used to having more car access, but we'd more or less sorted it out. Emily didn't complain about driving me places, and I didn't tell Mum and Dad how much of her paycheque she was setting aside for her own vehicle instead of next year's tuition.

"You can take it now," Mum said. "Consider it a birthday present."

"I'll text Jen while you grab your stuff," Mags offered, passing her empty plate to my dad's outstretched hands. "Thanks again for the waffles."

"I still think we should draw straws for who has to clean the waffle maker," Dad griped. Emily and I both took off from the table like a shot, and Mum laughed.

I went upstairs to my room and dumped my backpack out on my bed. It was mostly empty at this time of year. There were only a few days of school left, and no one was assigning much in the way of homework. I stuffed a hoodie and a clean pair of socks in the bottom—Louise's farm was reasonably clean, but one could never be too careful—and tossed my phone on top, along with a bottle of sunscreen, because I was one of those dark blonde girls who got scorched. That was all I needed for a Sunday afternoon with my friends.

Mum had given me the car for the day carelessly, but it was sticking in my throat for some reason. She'd done it because it was my birthday, but also because I was a good girl. Amelia and her sister had been a good girls, too. And the only thing her sister had done was drive Amelia to London. What was the point of being good if you could lose it so quickly, for something you hadn't done or for something you needed to do to keep your life intact? And why the hell was Adam Pedersen still a golden boy, when it had been just as much his doing?

I knew the answer, and it only made me more annoyed. I didn't say much as Mags and I left, or when we picked up Jen from her driveway four houses over. I just drove, both hands on the wheel and checking my blind spots every fifteen seconds, while Mags filled Jen in. Mags could tell something was wrong, and by the time we got to Louise's house, she was chewing on her lip. Jenny's car was already parked by the barn.

"I want to break something," I said, putting the car in park and turning off the engine. It hung there between the three of us, missing two sides, but finally spoken out loud.

"Me too," said Mags.

"Well, it's your birthday," Jen reminded me. "I'm sure we can figure something out."

2.

Maddie Carter

I knew Jen probably meant shooting tin cans or throwing rocks at the dead tree at the back of the Jantzis' apple orchard, but all I could think about was that giant new stone out the front of St. Brigid's. I hadn't seen it, but I had a rough idea what it looked like. Mags said it was black and grey, and looked like a gravestone, only there was nothing underneath it. That probably meant it was basalt. Basalt was too heavy to break on my own.

I watched Mags climb the ladder, her red curls shifting as she hauled herself up each rung. There was a perfectly good staircase on the other side of the barn, but it was *the other side of the barn*, so we always climbed. It gave the whole rumpus room a tree house/ clubhouse feel that we liked. The 4-H groups always came through the main door and used the stairs, and somehow that made our room different, even though it was the exact same physical space.

Louise had blown up about a hundred balloons and just turned them all loose in the rumpus room. They covered the Ping-Pong table and wafted gently from beanbag chair to beanbag chair, crashing into each other like very, very slow curling rocks every time one of us swatted at them. It was low effort and silly and fun, and I wanted to appreciate them, but I was having a hard time pretending it was just like any other party. The worst part was that I loved the rumpus room. It had been ours since grade

eight, and we'd never had to fight Louise's brothers for it, because
once Aaron had started working on the decrepit second house,
Paul bugged him instead of us.

"You can pop them all, if it'll make you feel better," Louise offered, after Mags had filled everyone in on the news and explained
my general rage.

"No, that's just messing up your work," I said, even though it
was tempting. I hit the balloon closest to me, and it ricocheted off
towards the air hockey table we only used for science experiments.
"It might make me feel better, but it wouldn't hurt the right people.
I want to do something permanent, but it can't just be random."

Stupid memorial stone, making me mad at dead babies. It wasn't
their fault, either, and I felt like we were being played against each
other so the grown-ups could win. I didn't like the idea that people
I was supposed to trust had been doing it to me my whole life.

"Well, you can't steal the stone," Mags said. "The corner is too
busy at night, and you'd need a truck *after* you got the stone off the
ground somehow."

"You read about kids breaking stones in cemeteries all the
time," Jenny suggested. "What about something like that?"

"Yeah, but those are the big stones with things on top of them,"
Mags said. "There's nothing to tip here. You'd need a sledge-
hammer, and it would be too noisy."

"Plus they'd just buy a new one," I pointed out. "And probably
use youth group money to teach the kids a lesson or something."

Mags scowled. That was exactly where the funds for the origi-
nal stone had come from, and now the youth group only had
snacks if someone's parents sent them in.

Louise glanced at the clock, and then went over to the mini-
fridge, tightening her blonde ponytail as she walked. She pulled

out my birthday cake and started counting out candles on the countertop. Of course Louise had made a cake. It was probably chocolate. She'd taught herself to make icing flowers, so the top was so covered in fancy buttercream that she had to take her time arranging the final display.

A few days ago, when my mother had produced an ice cream cake from the freezer, my life had seemed less complicated. The closest Dairy Queen was forty-five minutes away, so in this case, a store-bought cake was a thoughtful expression of time and effort. Mum had put sparklers on that cake, and instead of blowing them out, I made my wish as I watched them burn down. The light was hypnotic, but I didn't forget to make a wish. Now, sitting in the converted barn at Louise's house, I couldn't even remember what I had wished for.

Jen got the lighter from a drawer, but instead of giving it to Louise, she brought it over to the area where we were sitting. Louise had already dragged a low table over for the cake, and Jen sat behind us like she was about to call a meeting to order.

"So we can't break it or steal it," Jen said. She reached up with her free hand and wrapped a lock of dark brown hair around it. Half the teaching faculty at Eganston Elementary had tried to break her of the habit, and none had come close to succeeding. "But we want to do something. So what are we going to do?"

"We?" Jenny asked. She looked around. "I mean, don't get me wrong, I also think it's a stupid rock, but what are we going to do about it?"

"That's what we need to find out," Jen said.

Jenny shook her head, but she was already making the face she made when a teacher said it was time to brainstorm.

"I think it should be something that lingers," Louise said,

setting the cake down on the table. "They want the stone to be something people see and think about all the time. We should do the same thing."

"That makes it even harder," I said, but I knew that she was right. When I'd said I wanted to hurt someone, I didn't mean a quick, sharp pain, over soon and forgotten immediately. I wanted something that sunk in.

"I have an idea," Mags said. She'd been quiet for a while. "I'll need Jenny to start coming back to youth group, though."

Jenny recoiled. Her parents' civil divorce had made church awkward enough, but when her younger sibling Char came out, it had become intolerable.

"Just for the summer," Mags spoke with the quickness of someone with a lot of negotiation experience. "We'll feed Uncle David some story about how you miss the community, and that you want to reconcile your feelings."

"Why in the world would *anyone* believe I'd go back there?" Jenny asked. She wasn't angry at Mags, and we all knew it, but she was still angry.

It was a totally valid question, and one I had been about to ask myself, though I was going to phrase it differently. But something in the way Jenny said it made me realize instantly that whatever Mags's plan was, it was going to work.

"Because you're a good girl," I said. It was almost like I was dreaming. "We're all good girls. It's why Louise's parents never check in on us while we're out here. It's why we were all allowed to drive with each other the moment we got our G2s. They'll believe it because you told them, and anyone who doubts you will believe Mags when she backs you up."

"All right." Jenny looked skeptical, but slumped back in her beanbag chair. I had given her enough to start with. "Explain the plan, Mags."

"They had to use an excavator to get the stone in," Mags said. "It tore up the lawn, so they put down new sod. The sod still has to be watered and, like, taken care of, because it hasn't put down enough roots yet. The gardening committee will be in charge of that over the summer. They had to ask for more volunteers."

"I am *not* joining a committee," Jenny said.

"You don't have to," Mags told her. "Davy MacGregor's grandparents have taken care of the grounds since, like, the drafting of Nicene Creed, but they're leaving at the start of July to go visit the missionary branch of the family in Paraguay. Their volunteers don't really know what they're doing, even though there's instructions. Youth group meets on Tuesday, and the gardening committee meets on Wednesday mornings. All we have to do is switch whatever they're using with something that'll kill the sod."

"Sod has to be cheaper to replace than the memorial stone," Jen said.

"With the right chemicals, we can make it so that nothing ever grows on that ground again," Louise said. "There are like ten things in the storeroom in this building that'll—"

"No," I interrupted. They all looked at me sharply. "No, I mean, we can't use your dad's farm supplies, Louise. We have to be smart about it. Mags and Jenny will cover for each other at youth group, but the rest of us have to be just as careful."

Louise and Mags immediately got into an argument about industrial-strength weed killer that the rest of us could only kind of follow. I let them sort it out and glanced at Jen and Jenny. They weren't following the conversation, either—Jenny's mum had substantial vegetable gardens on the farm they rented, but she was 100 percent organic—and they looked keyed up anyway.

"We're really going to do this?" I asked. "You're really going to do this for me?"

"We're doing it for *us*," Louise said. "But it's your birthday."

Jen handed her the lighter, and she lit each of the seventeen candles she'd managed to artfully arrange on top of the heavily decorated cake. They didn't sing, but we could all feel a hum of excitement in the air. Jenny pushed the cake plate across the table to me with a smile on her face. Mags grabbed my hand and squeezed it.

I leaned forwards and blew the candles out.

3.

Maddie Carter

There were still a lot of details we had to figure out. Most of them were related to logistics, but since the garden committee had literally posted a schedule of sod care and maintenance including the chemicals to be applied on the church bulletin board, we had a good start. The more personal details were more daunting. Char might be angry when Jenny told them she was going back to church, for starters. We didn't want to put them through anything else—or any of the Hoernigs, for that matter. We were all on our second pieces of cake by the time Mags came up with a reasonable solution.

"Tell them I begged you," Mags said. "That you're just doing it for me, because otherwise I'd be all by myself in a gross church basement with a bunch of fourteen-year-olds, because all the sixteen-year-olds have jobs."

"It has the benefit of being true," Louise pointed out.

"Or I could just tell them the actual truth," Jenny said. She still sounded uncomfortable.

We all considered it for a moment. I could tell Emily before she went back to school. Mags could tell Aaron when he got home from his summer co-op at the agricultural college. Char would probably be thrilled.

"We can't," Jen said, finally. We all knew it was the best call. "We can't tell anyone, ever. It has to be a complete secret."

Jenny sighed and nodded.

"I don't think we should write anything down, either," she said. "No texts or emails, or even a to-do list. Just talking."

"What about internet search history?" Mags asked. "If we can't use the stuff our parents have, we'll have to Google for the commercial equivalents."

There was a long moment of silence, and then Louise made a face.

"Spit it out," Jenny said. "This is going to be uncomfortable anyway, so you might as well."

"Mags, we could ask your grandpa," Louise said, so quietly we barely heard her.

David Shropshall Sr. had been a pillar of all of our childhoods. His wife, Mags's grandmother—also named Magdalen, because: tradition—helped out with the steadily increasing number of Sharpe children in the main house, and we spent a lot of time with him to get away from the babies. It had been his farm before Mags's mom had taken it over, and he spent his retirement summers chasing five little girls around the woodlot, pretending to be whatever villain Louise was obsessed with that particular week. He'd started showing signs of dementia when we were in grade six, the little things, like forgetting his glasses or why he'd gone to the grocery store. By the time we started grade eight, he didn't remember anyone, except sometimes he mistook Mags for his wife or daughter.

The Sharpes talked about all the usual solutions: moving him into the main house and sending Mags to live with her grandmother across the yard, hiring someone to live in—all that sort of thing. The problem was that David was a wanderer, and the country wasn't safe for a man who knew he was a farmer, but couldn't remember how. In the end, they'd had to put him in a nursing home, which made none of them happy. Mags, David (the third), and Colin visited pretty regularly after school, bringing Elsie or Clara in turns. Teddy—the youngest of the six—only went on weekends, with Mags's mum and dad. Mags's grandma was there from breakfast to bedtime, knitting or reading, or talking with the other patients' family members.

"He'd definitely know what to use," Mags admitted. She was trying to sound detached, but her voice caught a bit. "And he'd never remember that he told us."

"I'm sorry," Louise said, still making herself small. "It's a mean idea."

"It's a good idea," Mags said. "But you're coming with me when we do it."

"I'll come, too," I volunteered quickly. I wanted to make it better. "Unless you think that would make it too crowded?"

"No," Mags said. "We always take him to the conservatory, and Grandma goes outside for a walk. We'll be fine."

We sat in a somewhat grim silence, finishing up the cake. I felt like I'd ruined my own birthday party. Both Jenny and Mags were on the spot with people they loved, and all for some stupid wish.

"You know," said Jenny, having scraped all the icing off of her plate, "even though this is weird and uncomfortable, I do feel better. We haven't even done anything yet, but I feel better."

"Honestly, the fact that it was so easy to come up with an idea makes me feel better," Louise said. "I feel like the past few weeks it's just been everyone nosing into everyone else's business, looking for mistakes."

"The looks I've got from people coming through my till at the grocery story are not subtle," Jenny said. "Like they're just waiting and wondering if I need a push."

"Well, you're going to fucking push," Jen said.

Jen and Jenny had both been members of the Child of a Single Mum Club until we were seven and Jen's mother married John Dalrymple, but Jen never forgot what it was like, and how everyone treated her when she "didn't have a responsible role model." At least Jenny's dad paid child support.

"You haven't ruined your birthday, is what they're trying to say," Mags said. "I know you're thinking it."

"I was," I admitted. The beanbag chair rustled as I shifted. "I didn't mean to drag you all into a life of crime because I was angry at a rock."

"It's a minor crime, at least," Louise pointed out. "We'll just go with whatever the girl equivalent of 'boys will be boys' is."

"I don't think there is one," Mags said. "The Latin for 'children' was translated into 'boys' in the 1750s."

"Why on earth do you know that?" Jen demanded.

"I like making adults uncomfortable," Mags said primly.

"When are you going to visit your grandpa?" Jenny asked. "Full offence, but I am not going back in that building—even the basement—until I have a reason."

"Mags and I both have spares third this week," Louise said. "We can go during lunch, and then after Maddie leaves we'll have enough time that I can help you get him resettled."

"We'll go on Wednesday," Mags said.

"Why not Monday?" I asked.

"Because I want to look at the supply closet at the church first," Mags said. "If there's stuff in there already we can use, then it's just a matter of switching bottles around."

"And not causing explosions," Jen added. "Some of those things don't play well with others."

"This is going to be so much to remember," Louise said. I could tell she was itching to make a list.

"Let's just take this one step at a time," Mags said. "We don't have to get everything done this week. We have all summer."

"It might actually be better if it takes all summer," Jenny said thoughtfully. "Imagine dead grass slowly spreading across the lawn, and the only source is the memorial stone. Like the opposite of when Mary statues cry or the Jesus bleeds."

"That means you have to go to youth group all summer," I reminded her.

"Yeah, but they've played mind games with my family for years," Jenny said. "I don't mind being patient to get something back."

A chime on Mags's phone went off, and she wrinkled her nose in disgust.

"Family dinner still on?" I asked.

"Yeah," she said. "At least it'll be interesting, right?"

She did not sound happy about it.

"Do you need a ride?" I asked.

"No," Louise said, her eyes gleaming with mischief. "Because Aaron is home this weekend, and he's going to be all white knight and sit through it with her."

"No, thank you," Mags said, as if Louise hadn't spoken. "Because Aaron is home this weekend, and he volunteered to be my white knight and keep me from doing a murder."

Her dignified answer did not stop the rest of us from bursting into giggles. Since five people is a lot, even when they are only girls, we'd spent a lot of our time as kids at either Louise's house or Mags's. Jenny's mum's camera store was in town, but there was always someone home at the other farms. Aaron started coming because he could drive Louise, Jen, and me to Mags's, and eventually he started staying because Mary and Theo Sharpe ran a full farm operation, and he could learn more with them than he could at home. He was always invited for dinner, and then it made sense for him to stay until our movie was done, and then, when we were in grade ten, Mags was somehow quietly dating Louise's older brother, and we all thought it was absolutely *hilarious*.

Just like that, it was a normal birthday again. A normal Sunday, even. The sick, hard feeling that had been clenching in my gut all day was lifted, and I kind of wanted another piece of cake. Louise broke out the pop and chips she'd brought over from the main house, along with a fruit tray in case any of us were feeling virtuous. Mags said her good-byes, and the rest of us wasted the afternoon talking about our upcoming exams and the fact that course selections were this week. When it was time to go home, we sorted the recycling and garbage, and Louise put all the strawberry hulls in a little container so that she could dump them in the compost on her way back to the house.

I dropped Jen off at the foot of her driveway at exactly six, and then barely touched the gas to make it down the block to my house. Dad was in the garden and made a big show of checking the car over for damage, but he couldn't stop laughing while he did it. We had dinner, all four of us sitting at the table, talking about nothing and everything at the same time. I finished up my homework, such as it was at this time of year, and brushed and flossed my teeth. I turned my light off at ten, and looked up at the glow stars I'd stuck to the ceiling when I was eight and afraid of the dark.

We were absolutely going to get away with it.

4.

Maddie Carter

On Wednesday when the bell rang for lunch, we headed for the doors by the library. Our English teacher waved at us as we left, but aside from that, no one asked us any questions. Mr. Rogman, the chemistry teacher, was waiting at the corner for his pizzas to be delivered—he sold slices for a dollar each every Wednesday to pay for field trips.

"No pizza today?" he asked.

"No," said Louise, who had never bought food at school in our entire lives.

"Have a good adventure, then," he said, which is what he always said instead of saying things like "see you tomorrow" or "see you after lunch because that's when you have chemistry."

"I'll be back in time for class," I assured him. He waved a hand dismissively.

"I'll mark you present either way," he said. "But if you don't make it back, you will miss the Flaming Ball of Science."

His favourite end-of-year trick was to submerge the gas tap hose in bubble water, collect a giant mass of bubbles on a metre-stick, and then light the whole thing on fire. It was neat, but I'd already seen it.

Like most kids who grew up in Eganston, I usually went to the nursing home a couple of times a year. In elementary school, the music teacher would take us caroling at Christmas, and there were always residents who gave out candy at Halloween. We never really went past the public rooms, but there was no doubt as to the nature of the place. It was always too warm, and half of the residents looked right through you.

When Mags's grandfather moved in, we all visited him pretty regularly at first. He shared a room with Dahlia Hastings's grandfather, so sometimes we saw her there, too. There was an unspoken agreement that we didn't really talk to her about it, especially not at school. Visiting was hard because David never acknowledged us. Even if he was the only one in the room at the time, he acted like we were there to visit someone else. Eventually we visited less and less, and the worst part was that Mags completely understood.

The room was airy today, because it was warm enough outside to open the windows. Dahlia's family had hung up a lot of greenery for Shavuot, so it even smelled pretty good. David was sitting in his upholstered chair from the farmhouse, and looked up when Mags said hello.

There was always a moment before you know how the visit was going to go. He'd look up, and then there'd be an awful pause, and then something would happen in his face. Sometimes his gaze stayed blank. Sometimes he panicked and called for the nurse. Sometimes he thought Mags was her grandma. Today was the fourth possibility: he thought we were random strangers who had come to visit him for no particular reason, and he was really pleased about it, because he was very bored.

"We've come to have lunch with you, David, if that's all right," Louise said. "The nurse's aide said she'd set up a card table in the conservatory and get you a tray."

"What are you three going to eat?" he asked, already changing his slippers for his shoes. His mobility was still mostly normal, which made him a flight risk, but he couldn't remember the code to get outside by himself.

"We've got our own lunches," Mags said. "We didn't want to cause any trouble."

"That's very sweet of you," David said. He was patting down his cardigan as he looked for something without knowing what it was he looked for. "These girls work very hard. I'm ready to go now."

Mags double-checked his shoes to make sure they were laced properly, and then helped him stand up. He barely needed a cane to walk, but the transfer was a little awkward out of a comfy chair. She kept her elbow linked with his, and we all headed down to the conservatory, slowly enough that David could pretend he was leading us—he was the host, after all—even though he had no idea where it was.

"Just pull the cord if you need anything," the nurse's aide said when we got there. She'd already gotten David's lunch, along with three extra slices of cake.

We thanked her, took our seats, and started eating. David started talking about dairy schedules, his default topic, and we didn't want to push him, so we just nodded at appropriate moments. When he paused, it wasn't the vague gap that his brain came up to with increasing regularity. He was still concentrating on something, it just wasn't cows anymore.

"The food here is quite good," he said. "But there is something wrong with this tuna sandwich. I don't know what, but there's something missing."

"It's pickles," Mags said, and held out the ziplock bag with the other half of her sandwich in it. "Do you want mine?"

"That is very kind of you," David said, and pushed his plate towards her.

Mags took the sandwich out and handed it to him. He took a bite and smiled so widely, it was like we were seven again, and he finally had us cornered in the hay barn.

"This is excellent," he said in the space between bites. "This tuna sandwich was made by someone who knows how. My wife was really good at tuna sandwiches." He paused and the vagueness returned. "I . . . don't know where she is."

Mags blinked several times, way too quickly, and Louise and I exchanged a look of helplessness. Even when it was good, it was awful.

"I've been trying to grow a kitchen garden this summer," Mags said, and none of us were at all surprised by the abrupt subject change. "It's started out pretty good, but the weeds are growing better than anything I planted on purpose."

"Ain't that always the way," David drawled. It was his exaggerated farmer voice instead of his normal one. It had always made us giggle when we were little. "I swear, some years I wish I'd planted milkweed and had a corn infestation."

"What did you do to stop the weeds?" Louise asked, shredding a string cheese into thread-thin strands instead of fidgeting.

"Well, you know, we had quite a bit of pesticide on hand," David said. "But when my grandkids came along, we decided to use something a bit softer in the kitchen garden."

Mags flinched. He didn't usually remember the grandchildren at all.

"That seems like a smart idea," I said. "What did you do?"

"We mixed up something from the kitchen, and put it in a spray bottle," David said. "Two parts salt and one part water."

Louise nodded, and I saw her mouth moving as she repeated it to herself several times because she couldn't write it down.

"But you have to be careful with it," David continued, "because if you use too much, it'll kill everything living in the dirt, and then nothing at all will grow."

That sounded like exactly what we were after, and it wasn't even going to be dangerous, or hard to get the supplies we needed. It was just a matter of figuring out how to do it.

"This is an excellent sandwich," David said, his attention diverting again. "The food here is quite good, but sometimes their tuna's not quite right, and today it's perfect. What am I supposed to do with all this cake?"

"We'll help," Mags said. He smiled brightly at her.

David talked about tuna sandwiches on loop for an hour. I hoped Mr. Rogman had actually marked me present, because I didn't leave Mags and Louise to go back to school. At 1:30, we walked him back to his room. He was fading fast by then, each sentence more vague and unrelated than the last. By the time Mags had him settled into his chair, he wasn't focusing on anything anymore. He just sat quietly with his hands folded on his lap, locked inside his own head. The nurses all smiled at us when we left. I took Mags's hand as Louise led the way down the sidewalk.

"You okay?" I asked. I rarely saw my own grandparents, but this was worse.

"No, but there's no good alternative," she said. She straightened her shoulders. "At least we found out what we need to know."

"Salt water," Louise said. "And he told us two things: what to make and how *not* to use it."

"Oh." Mags brightened. "You're right. Not only will we kill the sod, but if we do it enough, nothing will ever grow there again."

"That would be extra creepy," I said, imagining the gardening committee trying to explain to the MacGregors how they'd accidentally cursed the lawn without their supervision.

"Almost biblical," Mags agreed. "There's got to be salt in the storeroom, and the committee uses watering cans at the front because the hose doesn't reach that far."

"They might have pretreated water, too." Louise turned around to walk backwards while she talked. "When my uncle put in sod, he watered it with something from the sod company. Dad said it was just a cash grab, but—"

"That's exactly the sort of thing the gardening committee would buy," Mags finished. She was back to being determined, best foot forwards, but when I squeezed her hand, she smiled.

Fourth period was music for me, Jen, and Jenny, so I tried to fill them in as quietly as I could before we split off to go sit in our sections. There were too many other kids jostling around, though, so all I managed to tell them was that we had an answer and it wasn't going to be difficult to carry out. I could tell they were dying for the details, but there wasn't enough time to be safe about it, so they had to wait.

I could feel them watching me as I put my bassoon back in its case while they disinfected their mouthpieces. As soon as the bell rang, everyone was off to their lockers so they'd catch their bus. Jen grabbed me and pulled all three of us into one of the soundproofed practice rooms.

"Well?" she demanded.

I told them everything, from the pickles to the salt, and by the time I was done, Jenny looked more determined than ever.

"I still don't love the idea of going back," she said. "But it's definitely a worthy cause."

"It means a lot to Mags," I said. Jenny was a force of nature when she was committed to something. I wanted that commitment to hurt as little as possible. "And to me."

"Now we just have to wait," Jen said. "By which I mean get through exams."

"But then it's summer," Jenny said. "And usually I'm a little pissed to be stuck in town, working at the berry farm again, but this year, I don't think it'll be so bad."

"Not for us, anyway," I said. "This year it's going to be good."

5.
Maddie Carter

The thing I will always remember about the summer after grade eleven is how incredibly normal it was. We finished our exams, and all of a sudden it was July. Louise and I were lifeguards at the Lions pool; Mags split her time between working for her parents and helping her grandma; Jen didn't have a job because her parents had planned four separate weeklong trips over their vacation (they both taught at the elementary school); and Jenny was at the berry farm during the early morning and back at her till at the grocery store in the evenings.

The only really strange part—and it wasn't strange to us—was that the new sod in front of St. Brigid's died. Despite the best efforts of the leaderless gardening committee—all of whom swore they'd followed their instructions to the letter—the new grass withered and died, turning brown and crunchy in the steamy July humidity, no matter how much they watered it. During the fourth week of July, the committee bought and planted new sod, rolling up the brown stuff like old carpet. The sod was green for about ten days, during which time they once again scrupulously followed the schedule of maintenance, and then it died, too.

Mags and Jenny had it down to an art. Every Tuesday, a slightly mystified Julia Hoernig would drop her daughter and Mags off at the church around 6:30. Mags always came early to set up the room, and Jenny had volunteered to help with the tables. There was almost always some kind of spill or mess that required a trip to the supply closet for the mop and bucket, or a roll of paper towels, and if it took them a little bit longer to fetch whatever they needed, no one cared.

One night in mid-July, Father Shropshall actually caught Mags in the supply room.

"I was terrified," Mags reported later that week, when we all met up. Since we couldn't text, we usually saved any updates for when we all got together. This week, it was Jen's house because her parents were at a party and we wanted to take advantage of their extremely large television for a movie night. "There wasn't even a mess to clean up this week. I was just in the room, salting the bottles."

"What did you do?" Jen asked. She set a bag of pretzels and two Tupperware containers of Bulk Barn M&M's down on the table so we could snack.

"I told him there was a mess to clean up, and while I was getting the bucket, I had noticed some equipment the gardening committee must have forgotten to put away," Mags said, carefully selecting one M&M in every colour. "He thanked me for being helpful. He said the gardening committee was under a lot of stress, so they would probably appreciate it."

"I'm glad it was you," Jenny said. "If I'd been fast enough to think of a cover story, I definitely would have laughed in his face when he thanked me."

"I don't know," Mags said, tossing back the red. "He is being super careful with you right now. I heard him talking to my dad about it, something like 'staying in touch with modern kids while still being faithful to tradition.' I think he thinks he's actually making headway with you. You could probably get away with even more than I can right now."

Jenny made a derogatory sound and ate a whole handful of M&M's at once. Then Louise started the movie, and we spent the next two hours making fun of the anachronistic costume choices.

All told, the plan had gone extremely well. The area around the memorial was always brown and dying. I did feel a little bad the week that Mrs. Abernathy donated several flats of flowers to be planted, because she didn't have a lot of money to spare, but by then, we'd salted the land like the Romans at Carthage. The flowers didn't even take ten days to die. The gardening committee blamed the early August heat, and decided to try fresh grass seed next.

"It's a shame, really," Mum said one night at dinner. "That memorial is ugly enough, and they can't even dress it up with flowers."

"Maybe the stone is toxic or something?" Emily asked. "I mean, beyond socially toxic, obviously."

"I think it would take longer for something to leach out of a rock," I said carefully. "We haven't had that much rain this summer."

"I never complain about just deserts," Mum said. "Unless they're happening to me, obviously."

When the grass seed failed to sprout, the gardening committee gave up for the season. They tilled everything, making another muddy mess in front of the church when we had a few days in a row of mid-August rain. They stirred in bagged compost, too, so it wasn't just an eyesore. Father Shropshall even came out on Wednesday to work with them and bless the ground.

A week later, with Jen home from camp and Jenny rained out from work at the berry farm, we spent a morning at my house,

crammed into my bedroom even though we didn't really fit anymore.

"It'll probably be fertile again next year, but we gave them two
months of stress," Jenny said. She lay back on the floor with her
legs up the wall, flexing her toes. "I was at the store when the committee members bought the compost, though, and they talked the
whole time about what a mystery it was."

"I managed to sneak a salt cellar out of the kitchen and dump
it in the holy water Uncle David made for the blessing," Mags admitted. Her arms were wrapped around a pillow as she sat against
my headboard.

For some reason, this seemed like the most audacious thing
we'd done, and all of us looked at her in shock.

"Are you fucking kidding me?" Jenny asked, craning her head
around somewhat ineffectually.

"It was in his office in a jug," Mags said. She shrugged like
blasphemy was her normal course of action. "It took me like a
minute."

"I love you," Jenny said.

"Shut up," Mags told her. "The ratios were all wrong, so it's
not actually going to kill anything. It's just symbolic."

"So's the fucking memorial," I said.

"We have more important things to think about," Louise said.
She was spinning around on my desk chair, but set a foot down to
stop herself when she spoke. "Jenny's birthday is the twenty-fifth,
and we have to schedule something, because everyone is all over
the place."

It was true. For the whole summer, all five of us had managed
to get together once a week, but it had always been for a short
period of time. I'd spent hours with Louise at the pool, and plenty

of time with everyone else, but this year it had been harder to orchestrate all five of us. None of us really wanted to think about that and what it meant going forwards. We'd always had different schedules and hobbies and interests. It had always taken a bit of organization to keep us all together, and while Louise lived for that sort of thing, this summer felt different.

"I want a six-hour block," Louise said, holding up a hand to stave off any protests. "I realize that is a long time, but that way if we end up with four or five hours, it'll still feel like an afternoon, you know?"

We did know. Lousie and I were clear in the mornings now that swimming lessons were over, but evening swim didn't end until eight. Mags was the most flexible, but someone would have to go get her. Jen volunteered to be the driver and general errand runner, because while her schedule was limited by her access to the family cars, she still had the most free time. Jenny's schedule was almost impossible, and it was her birthday.

"The grocery store always lets me book my birthday off, so I'll be done at the berry farm at two, and free for the rest of the day," she said.

Jen texted her mother immediately, asking for the car, and Louise and I looked at the pool schedule. By some miracle, we were both off at four that day.

"Oh, that is awesome," Louise said, realizing that everything was going to line up. "We'll have from, like, 4:15 to curfew!"

"4:30," I said. "I hate showering at the pool, so I have to go home first."

"Fine, fine," Louise said. "You can come earlier and set up, Jen."

Jen's phone beeped, and she checked it quickly. "Mum said I

can have the car. I told her to write it down and everything," she said. "So yes, Mags and I will come over early, and if we need anything lifted or carried, Mags can ask Aaron."

Mags grabbed a sock from my laundry basket and threw it at Jen.

"Someday you are going to figure out how to talk to Dahlia Hastings, and I will be absolutely *merciless*," Mags said.

"Well, maybe I will," Jen said. She threw the sock back, but I intercepted it and returned it to the basket.

Mags checked the clock and sighed. It was almost three, and that's when her mum was going to pick her up. Jenny had to leave, too, because she had the evening shift at the grocery store.

"At least when school starts, we'll be legally required to be in the same building," Louise grumbled.

"When you say it like that, it almost sounds worth it," Jenny said.

"I'm just glad my parents will be legally required to be in an entirely different building," Jen said, twisting her hair around her finger.

Everyone went downstairs to get their shoes, and I waved them off from the door. Louise was always planning something, but I never thought to ask if Jenny had already been planning, too, and holding it close until we were all together in the security of the rumpus room in the barn. In hindsight, none of us should have been surprised. My birthday wish had cost Jenny a lot, even if she was satisfied with the results.

On August 25th, we made our way to Louise's. My hair was dripping, and Louise was still wearing her bathing suit. Jenny had had time to clean up after work, and Mags and Jen had hung streamers and made a playlist. When Louise set Jenny's cake down in front of her, Jenny took the lighter out of her hand.

"Guys, I've been thinking," Jenny said. She rolled the lighter around her palm, but there was plenty of fire in her eyes. "I want to make a wish."

SECOND WISH:

Slander

(OR: JENNY'S 17TH BIRTHDAY)

6.

Jenny Hoernig

The thing you have to understand about me and Mags is that we oldest child very differently. Mags has way more siblings, but she also has three reliable adults (four, before her grandpa got sick). For her, being responsible is being home so that if anything comes up that she can deal with, it gets dealt with. For me, being responsible means getting my driver's license the moment it's legal so I can help Mum with the driving, and getting a job so I can help with the family budget.

The first sign that my mum should have left my dad was my sister Adah. We're Irish twins (not the nicest term, I know, but it helps me stay angry at my dad). We were born in two different calendar years, so it doesn't sound as bad, but no one should give birth twice that close together, and it almost killed my mum. Dad didn't care about that, or his two babies. He had stuff to do. By the time Dottie was born (barely a year after Char, who was only two years younger than Adah), my mother had four children under the age of five, and somehow found the courage to kick him out. Our lives have been hand-me-downs and "Oh, why don't you take the leftovers home, I'll just wrap them up for you" ever since.

When I got my first job—babysitting, of course, because I was twelve—it was helping Mags look after her horde of younger siblings during the summer. In hindsight, it was a total setup. By the end of the second week, my siblings had been invited to come with me, and we stayed there for breakfast, lunch, and dinner. Mags's grandma was in the house with us like 90 percent of the time, but I still got paid five dollars an hour. Mum was able to be at the store until six, which meant she didn't have to hire part-time help. The summers we were thirteen and fourteen were a little more complicated. Mags's grandpa now took all of her grandma's attention, Char came out as nonbinary and we left the church, and we had Mags's baby brother Teddy to take care of. Mags just rolled with it, but it was too many people for me, so at the end of the summer, when I turned fifteen, I applied for a Social Insurance Number and a job at the grocery store.

At first I didn't understand why everyone was so upset. I was making twice as much money, and no one had to change diapers. I got to see my friends more often, because I wasn't stuck out in the country all the time. But we didn't get to eat the casseroles that Mags's dad made anymore, and Adah had to be in charge of our siblings at home, where we had fewer toys. I offered to quit and go back, but my mother only sighed, looked at her bank spreadsheet, and said it was okay as long as I gave her three of my thirteen dollars an hour. I agreed, and Mum got a Netflix subscription to help Adah maintain order.

We needed a lot of help, but we were a team. I made sure to channel any resentment I felt about giving up my money and time towards deserving people (my dad, Father Shropshall, and every person at the grocery store who *still* asked me how my *sisters* were doing). We were doing okay.

And then I told my mother that I was going back to youth group.

"Why?" she asked, slumping over the kitchen table. I had to

wait until my siblings were gone, obviously, and that had taken some doing, so it was the night before the first meeting when I finally had time to tell her.

"Mags asked me to," I told her. As Louise suspected, it was much easier to say something that was actually the truth. "She's going to be all by herself with a bunch of sweaty boys if I don't go, and they mostly just hang out, anyway. If Mags is there by herself, she'll always end up cleaning up after everyone."

If there was one thing my mother understood, it was being left with the cleanup.

"If it makes you feel better, I will do my best to set a terrible example," I said. I wished so badly that I could tell her why I was doing this. I knew she'd approve of it. "And aggressively ask for people's pronouns when I meet them."

That made her laugh. She straightened up and looked at me with that patented Mum "Where has the time gone?" look. "That does make me feel better," she said. "But I am not making one fucking Rice Krispie square for those people."

"Neither am I," I told her. "I gave Mags very specific terms."

Telling Char was approximately a million times worse. They understood, just like Mum did, but I knew I had hurt them, and that made me so angry. Fortunately, I had a great place for my anger to go: right into the sod around the goddamn abortion memorial.

It was a heady rush, damaging something that was important to people who had damaged my family. I knew that I was technically doing this for Maddie—and Amelia—but it was still a nice feeling every time I put one of the contaminated bottles back on the shelf. I never actually saw the gardening committee at work, but I liked to imagine them getting more and more frustrated as the summer went on, unaware that whatever they were using was what was actually killing the grass.

Outside of that, the summer was pretty normal. By which I mean I was fucking exhausted all the time. I had to be at the berry farm by six in the morning, and that meant I worked closing at the grocery store, which was 10:30 p.m. by the time we cashed out. I didn't work both places every day, but I did it enough that I was pretty sure I could have driven from the farm to the store with my eyes closed. Adah worked at the berry farm, too, now, and we were always scheduled at the same time because my boss was not an asshole. We shared a car, or we would when Adah got her G2, so it was handy that we always worked at the same time.

Still, I was counting down the days to September. I didn't even like school that much, but at least it started at nine. I'd be driving everyone this year, but not even that could lessen my excitement. I just wanted to not have mosquito bites and not have to worry about ticks until next spring's asparagus season.

I hadn't forgotten about my birthday, exactly, before Louise brought it up. I just hadn't spent a lot of time thinking about it. As soon as she did, though, my brain started turning the idea over. I watched Louise make a list with the fervour of someone who hasn't been *allowed* to make a list for a while, listened while Jen and Mags effectively took over the planning once we'd come up with a time, and thought about something I didn't usually waste time thinking about, because it wasn't relevant: what I wanted for my birthday.

My mum did her best. We were never hungry, and we were never cold, but there were definitely things we didn't have. I was lucky, because the girls always shared things without making a big deal of it, but I know my siblings—especially Char, who was stuck with whatever hand-me-downs Adah and I were finished with—felt the bite. We got presents for our birthdays, but they were usually practical or small.

Maddie's birthday wish hadn't cost us any money. She had felt an injustice, and we had helped her deal with it. And, yeah, I had some personal investment in making Father Shropshall miserable (or at least confused), but it was still something we had done for her. I didn't feel like I was owed something, but as my party was planned around me, I couldn't help but wonder if I could ask them to do it again, this time for me.

I considered it carefully all the way to my birthday party. I thought about everyone who had made me mad or done something to my siblings, and decided that that was too personal. We read a book called *Strangers on a Train* in grade ten. I hated reading ancient books because the authors were always like "Oh, here's some queer subtext, and also I went on to write the first lesbian novel with a happy ending," which would get me excited, and then I'd look them up on Wikipedia and find out that they were horrible people and our teachers just hoped we wouldn't notice. Anyway. The book was about two strangers who meet on a train and agree to outsource their plans to murder family members to each other. And obviously the story was not a great example of success, but the key idea of doing jobs *for each other* was definitely something that I could work with.

As soon as I expanded my thinking, I found a target immediately. For a small town that was supposed to be one of the "nice" ones, Eganston had a lot of injustice boiling just below the surface. I thought about what we could do and how we could do it. I wondered if it was ethical, or if it was a step too far. I let myself think about what would happen if we were successful.

And then, at my birthday party, I sat there as Louise set the cake down in front of me. It was banana cream pie–flavoured, because Jen had been feeling experimental, and Mags had gotten sparklers instead of candles for the top, which was why Louise waited until it was set down to light them.

Before she could, I reached forwards and took the lighter out of her hand. They all looked at me, surprised, but I saw in Maddie's face the moment she realized what I was going to do. It was a flash of understanding in her eye, and then a small smile.

"Guys, I've been thinking," I said. "I want to make a wish."

It took a second to land, and then Mags leaned forwards.

"Like Maddie's?" she asked.

"Yeah," I told them. "Like Maddie's."

The five of us looked at each other, more than a decade and a half of not always needing words to get the point across.

"All right," said Jen. "Let's hear it."

7.

Jenny Hoernig

A thing to understand about Eganston Central Secondary School is that it is decidedly middling at all things. We have a decent tech program, okay sports teams, a run of good music and drama teachers, and an otherwise competent faculty, but we're not shiny or new. It is customary, for example, to check the names in the front of any textbook you receive for a class, and if a classmate's parent's name is written in the cover, you give them the book. Nothing has been repainted since 2002, and no one in living memory can recall the tennis court (singular) having a net.

The cafeteria makes great chocolate chip cookies, though.

Anyway, every once in a while, someone does something really flashy, like make a provincial hockey team, but aside from that, no one ever really does anything that gets recognition above the conference level.

Isobel Johnson was one of our exceptions. She had been sick a lot when we were in elementary school, but by the time she got to ECSS—a year ahead of us—she was doing fine. In grade nine phys ed, she discovered volleyball, and from that moment it was on. Isobel was tiny, but she was quick and she had uncanny aim. She was a natural setter, and our volleyball coach (who actually knew what he was doing) encouraged her to play. Her mum actually drove her to Stratford—forty-five minutes per way—three times a week to play club volleyball. As she got better, the whole team kind of grew around her. By the time they were in grade twelve, they actually kind of had a chance to maybe make it to provincials.

I was in grade eleven and my first year as a senior when everything fell apart. I'd really been looking forward to playing with Isobel, even though I knew I'd be on the bench for most of the season, because our coach was playing to win. We'd started practice after Christmas break, and after two weeks, we were really coming together. We were three days out from our first game when Trevor Harrow decided to be, in Jen's words, a fucking asshole.

Trevor and Isobel had dated on and off since grade ten, and she had finally dumped him for good just after the Halloween dance. Trevor was out, and he knew it, and so he decided to get some revenge.

I know more of the facts than most people, because my mum and Isobel's mum are close. I think Trevor was just trying to force Isobel to reveal her medical condition, but he couldn't even do that properly.

Instead, he told his dad, our principal, that he'd seen Isobel doing steroids while they were dating. For some incomprehensible reason, Mr. Harrow decided to believe him, and called in Isobel to discuss it. Maddie had been in the guidance office filling out a summer camp application, and she'd heard him yelling about it. Mr. Harrow hadn't even closed the door. Isobel swore up and down that she hadn't taken steroids, and then Mr. Harrow insisted that she prove it by taking a drug test.

Nothing, not even common sense or an intervention from Isobel's parents, would change Mr. Harrow's mind. He was one of those men who couldn't imagine ever stepping back after he'd asserted some measure of petty authority. Either she took the test, or she was off the team.

Isobel failed the drug test.

Trevor had wanted to embarrass her into revealing that she had Turner syndrome, but instead she just took the fall. I knew about it, because my mum had stopped her mum from trying some crazy homeopathy, but as far as anyone else, Isobel kept the secret very close. The medication she took to treat her heart condition was what the test picked up, but as far as everyone knew, Isobel had cheated, and now she was going to pay for it.

The kicker—and something that Isobel did not know and I only knew about because her mother had hissed it to my mother over coffee and tears at like midnight just before the volleyball season was supposed to start—was that in desperation, Mrs. Johnson *had* told Mr. Harrow the truth. He told her that since Isobel couldn't prove she hadn't cheated, it didn't matter. She had failed the drug test, and she was lucky he hadn't expelled her.

(When my mother pointed out that that would have been very illegal, Mrs. Johnson had snapped her reading glasses in half.)

Mr. Harrow was gone, having failed upward to superintendent, but Trevor had come back for a fifth year of high school because his grades weren't great and he wanted to play hockey again.

Before I handed the lighter back to Louise, I told them what I thought we should do.

"Trevor Harrow," I said. Jen actually growled.

"That fucking fucker," said Jen, stabbing her plastic cake fork into the beanbag chair so hard it snapped a tine.

"What do you have in mind?" Mags asked.

"It's vaguely unethical and possibly ableist," I said. "But it's also turnabout, and that might make it fair play?"

They all looked a little bit uncomfortable, but Mags got over it first. She'd seen me at youth group every week this summer, and she knew what it had cost me.

"All right," she said.

"Trevor put Isobel in a position where she had to prove a negative," I said. "And he went after her medical history. He probably just wanted to embarrass her, but instead he gave her six straight months of hell and took away the thing she was best at. Trevor's not really good at anything, but we can definitely give him hell."

"You want to give him a medical condition he can't prove he doesn't have," Maddie said.

"It's not going to be quite as easy as ruining the memorial," I told her. "I've only had a few days to do research, but—"

"*Online?*" said Louise.

"No," I said. "I went to the library and flipped through a medical dictionary."

"Oh." Louise leaned back in her seat.

"Thanks," I said, but I was grinning. She was only looking out for us. "I haven't figured out all the details, but I want to frame him for using steroids."

"How would that even work?" Jen asked. She was looking enthusiastic at the idea, though.

"We steal his school log-in, and then look up a bunch of stuff about how to avoid being detected while you're using steroids," I said, like it was easy. "Then we make sure the right people find out about it."

"That definitely seems fair, considering what he did," Mags said. "But they'll just make him take a test, and he'll be okay after that."

"We have to make it look like he was planning to, then," I said. "And make sure everyone is furious at him, regardless how the test comes back."

"This is going to be really mean," Louise said. "But I have to admit, it sounds like justice."

I thought about all those times Isobel's mum had come over to our house while they were trying to get a diagnosis. The helplessness she felt at having failed her baby girl genetically and then failed her again by being unable to help her defend herself. I imagined what that conversation with the principal must have been like, how she broke her glasses because she was so mad and powerless.

And I thought about Isobel. I thought about every single loss we had that season, and how each of them was Trevor's fault. I thought about Chelsie, our backup setter, who I'd found crying in the change room more than once because she wasn't a good enough replacement. I thought about how the game that Isobel loved so much had been taken away from her, even though she hadn't done anything wrong. And I thought about all the shit that she endured between the end of January and the day she graduated, because even telling the truth, which she owed to no one, wouldn't have made it better.

"Did you know that the least amount of money superintendents make is $160,000?" Mags said. "The most a teacher can make is $90K, and that's fifteen years in."

"Jesus," I said. "Now I hope we really catch Mr. Harrow in the cross fire."

"Yeah," Mags said. "Is it just going to be rumours, or what?"

"Definitely to start with," I said. "But we got our class schedules this week, and if nothing changes, three of us have biology first semester. I know there's an independent study unit in grade twelve bio, so I propose we incorporate that somehow."

"That way it'd be harder to trace the rumours back to us, because everyone will be doing research at the same time," Maddie pointed out. "It's just going to take a while."

"I think that's okay," Louise said, leaning back in her chair. "Don't get me wrong, the sod was a good first step, but it was pretty easy to pull together. Taking our time on this one makes sense. We really want it to stick."

"Same rules as last time," Jen said, a coil of hair springing free against her neck. "No internet, no texts or emails. We have to remember things and we only talk in person."

I met Maddie's gaze. I understood how she had felt two months ago when she had voiced her frustrations and we had just stepped up to help. Because now they were doing the same for me. It wasn't nice and it wasn't good, but it felt very, very right.

"Well, I'm glad that's settled, then," I said. I offered up the lighter. "Now, will somebody *please* light the cake?"

8.

Jenny Hoernig

The worst part was waiting. We got right down to it when it came to poisoning the ground outside the church, but the independent study unit in bio wasn't until the first week in October, so we had four weeks to sit there and live life as normal. If I hadn't walked into the classroom five days a week and felt a rush of anxiety, I'd probably have forgotten, but instead we waited and waited and waited. Trevor didn't even make it hard to steal his log-in. His password was "jockstrap."

The world kept going, of course. We were in the last year of high school now, and there were things that needed to be considered. About thirty kids were going to graduate from ECSS that year, and the guidance counsellor met with each of us in September to talk about our plans. Because I had been thinking about this since grade ten, my meeting went pretty quickly. The guidance counsellor called up the prerequisites for the course I wanted to enroll in, a college program that will turn me into a lab tech in two short years.

"Well, you're definitely going to be overqualified for college," Mrs. Kelly said, comparing the list with my transcript. "In fact, you have the marks to get into a university program for biology. Why don't you do that?"

"Because I want to be a lab tech," I said.

"Yes, but you *could* be a biologist," she replied. "You'd still work in a lab if you wanted, but you'd have a lot more potential opportunities."

I bite my tongue. The college is forty-five minutes away, which means I can live at home and drive in. That alone will save a tonne of money. College tuition is way cheaper than university fees, and the program is half as long, with the option for two summer co-ops. At the end of four years of university, I'd have a degree that I *might* be able to use to get a job. At the end of two years of college, I'd have a certificate, job experience, and connections. And if I decided I wanted a university degree later, there were always a bunch of grants for older students.

"I know," I told her. "But I want to be a lab tech."

"At least go on a campus tour at Western," she said. "It's actually closer than Fanshawe, which I assume is the college you've picked."

I weighed my options. A free trip to London usually meant a stop at McDonald's on the way home, or even Swiss Chalet.

"Fine," I told her. "I'll go look at the campus."

"Excellent," she said, definitely patting herself on the back for helping another wayward teen live up to her potential. "I'll put you on the list and let you know when the trip has been organized."

She signed my green slip, writing the time down so messily I could have stayed in the cafeteria for an hour and still used her note when I went back to class.

"I know that it can be hard sometimes," she said with a smile. "You want to help your mother and you want to help your siblings. I know you're being practical, and I really do admire that, but I want you to see the other choices, too, just in case it shakes something loose, okay?"

"Okay," I said, almost shocked into silence by her perception.

But then again, it's a small town, and it's not like she doesn't know both Adah and Char, *and* she's aware that Dottie will be along next year. Plus she always remembers the pronouns. "Thank you."

"That's what they pay me for." Mrs. Kelly laughed.

There were about fifteen minutes remaining in second period, and I had left all of my stuff in the music room, so I made my way back. I walked down our so-called Hall of Fame, where the admin hung pictures of students who did big, exciting things with sports. There were five whole pictures, and none of them were for school teams. I stopped at the end, where the picture of the volleyball team would have hung, if we'd made it to OFSAA. For the first time, it didn't make me angry. It made me feel determined instead.

Jen was putting my mouthpiece in the disinfectant when I got back to class, because that's what friends are for.

"Your saxophone is on your seat," she said, swirling the black plastic around in the pan a bit before shaking it off and handing it to me. "Did you decide your future?"

"Yeah, but Mrs. Kelly wants me to go and look at Western anyway," I told her.

"Ugh." Jen made a face. She also had to apply to Western, even though she wanted to go literally anywhere else. She'd gone to the same elementary school and high school as both her parents, and she was determined not to go to their university, too. "On the bright side, Mrs. Heskie usually does that trip, and last year she took them to an Indian restaurant. For culture."

That would be much better than Swiss Chalet. Mum made Indian food sometimes because it was cheap to make a lot of it, and even the vegetarian stuff was really filling, but there was only so much you could learn from Google. An actual restaurant would be very cool.

"At least we'll have each other," I said.

Maddie bounced over from the woodwind shelves. I put my saxophone in the case and closed the latches. Like everything else in the building, the musical instruments were old and very used. Concert band was mostly for fun, and music class was an extension of it. Three years ago, some boy had gone to university for piano. They'd put one of the pianos in a practice room for him, exclusively, so that he could practice through lunch and any of his spares. Sometimes, he would even be in there playing while thirty grade nines tortured ourselves through "Hang on Sloopy" in the main room. Another flash in the pan.

The bell rang, and we headed for our lockers. They were less spread out than usual because this year we'd all been assigned to opposite sides of the same hall. Maddie and I went down to the cafeteria, and Jen peeled off to join the others at Reach for the Top practice, which Mads and I agreed was too stressful.

"So, next week," Maddie said when we had settled in at the end of our table.

"Yeah," I said. "Next week."

We had a biology test on Friday, and that meant a new unit on Monday: independent study. None of us had changed our minds. If anything, watching Trevor Harrow walk through the halls trying to intimidate grade nines made us want to hurt him even more. He left us alone completely, like he didn't even know we existed. So much the better, but it was very telling how he chose his targets. All of his friends had graduated, and he should have been alone, but instead he'd kept his seat at the table—literally—and the other boys on the hockey team raced to sit beside him.

"Do you think Mags is going to want to do this?" Maddie

asked. She unwrapped her sandwich and traded half with me without conversation.

"Of course," I said. I lined up my salami and cheese next to my salmon, and decided to save the salmon for last. "We all agreed."

"No, I mean when it's her birthday," Maddie explained. She started with the salmon. "Like, when it's November and it's her turn."

I hadn't thought about it. I ate a few bites and wondered what sort of vengeance Mags would wreak if she had the chance to.

"Yeah," I said. "I think she will."

"It's too bad we can't put 'organized overlapping events with a lot of details' on our résumés," Maddie said.

"I'm pretty sure Louise is going to anyway," I said. "But she'll hide it under her work with Students' Council."

It only took us about fifteen minutes to eat. We didn't stay in the cafeteria when we were done. Mr. Harrow had spent two years trying to enact a "caf or library, only" policy at lunchtime, but it had failed spectacularly because none of the teachers would enforce it. Usually we all ended up sitting in a circle on the floor by Mags's locker (because it was on an end), playing cards or talking. On Wednesdays we had jazz band. Jen did so many clubs that she almost never ate lunch in the cafeteria at all. In any case, it worked in our favour since the only people in the library at lunch were the ones who needed to be there. We would have no trouble getting a study carrel with a desktop computer, and we'd be able to frame Trevor without doing the research during class time, when we'd be more exposed because Mr. Rogman actually cared about what we were researching.

Maddie put her lunch bag away and got out her backpack

again. Another one of Mr. Harrow's failed policies was to stop us from bringing our backpacks to class. Last year's grade twelves had solved that one in a week by malicious compliance. They went through about four hundred late slips running from the third floor to the first floor to the second floor to get books. I know for a fact that the girls were planning something gross and period-related if they had to escalate, but it never came to that.

(My absolute favourite of Mr. Harrow's ridiculous policies was that he wanted us to sing the national anthem instead of just standing for it. He got rid of all our pretty instrumental versions and replaced them with an honest-to-God *tape* of sung versions. I don't think he listened to it first, though, because one of them was the one the Nylons recorded in 1989. The first time it played, I was in math class, and we all thought we were having a stroke. It was the only version of the "O Canada" we ever actually sang along with, and we always sang it at the top of our lungs.)

Anyway, we did have a test on Friday, so Maddie and I studied until the bell rang, because we were nerds and also good girls. Mags came to her locker to get her stuff, and the three of us headed to biology together. This time, when I walked into the room, it wasn't anxiety that I felt. It was expectation.

9.

Jenny Hoernig

While I spent the first month of school waiting for a unit in biology, Char was trying to settle into grade nine. It's not the easiest thing to do under normal circumstances—most of the hazing and "orientation" practices have been outlawed, but there's still spirit week, where all the hazing happens under teacher supervision. Char had come out of elementary school with a couple of really good friends, but since five elementary schools fed into ECSS, they had to explain themself over and over again.

There was nothing Adah or I could do about it. Nothing I could do would make Char's introduction any smoother. For a while, I thought they were doing okay. Then I noticed that Adah had let them sit in the front seat every day for a week while I drove us all to school, and I knew that something was up.

"You want to talk about it?" I asked one afternoon in the parking lot while we waited for Adah to extract herself from her incredibly chatty friends and get in the car.

"No," Char said.

"I thought you were going to try out for basketball, is all," I said. "I was expecting to shuffle around the driving schedule with Mum."

"I decided not to," Char said. They looked down at their hands.

"Is it a change room thing?" I asked. "Because Mum will kill someone if it's a change room thing."

"No," Char said. "I decided not to try out for the girls' team, that's all."

God, they were so much braver than I was. I hated that they had to be, even while I was very proud of them.

"You're going to play for the boys," I said. "When did you decide that?"

Char laughed. They were only fourteen, and the sound was so much older than that. Another thing I hated.

"Mr. Rogman started grade nine science with genetics this year," they said. "It's fascinating how a grown man can talk about sex organs and sweet pea chromosomes in a room full of teenagers, but *I'm* the one he has to talk around."

"Did he ask stupid questions?"

"No," they said. "He ignored me completely. I was in the front row. He didn't make eye contact even once."

"Do you want me to talk to him?" I asked. It wasn't Char's job to educate every ignorant person in Eganston, even the ones who were well-meaning and genuinely curious.

"Nah, it's fine," Char said. "Having grown-ups be afraid of me is kinda novel. I'm going to see if I can take advantage of it somehow. And to be perfectly honest, I got the impression that he's avoiding me because he's terrified of making a mistake. Once he gets into the swing of it, he'll be fine. *And* he'll feel bad, which I can exploit."

Adah came out the double doors, surrounded by her friends, and waved to us. It always took them a few minutes to say good-bye. Sometimes there was hugging involved, even though she'd see all of them again tomorrow.

"As long as nothing's bad," I said. "I . . . I know it hurt when I went back to youth group this summer, and if I can make it up to you, I will."

"Mags needed you," Char said. "We left, but she can't, and I know it makes her uncomfortable. David and I talk about it sometimes."

Before I could ask anything about their conversations with Mags's brother, Adah finally opened the rear door and slid into her seat. She was talking a mile a minute, and I heard the word "steroids" twice before I registered what she was talking about. Then I had to swallow what I am sure was a smug, incriminating smile.

"I knew he wasn't smart, but researching on school computers is extra stupid," Adah said, fastening her seatbelt.

"I don't like it when people have rumours spread about them," Char said. "But at least Trevor is an asshole."

I nodded, and navigated the car out of the lot. I wanted Char to feel safe at school, and knowing they might be prey to the rumour mill at any moment definitely sucked.

"Some people are just jerks," Adah said.

I couldn't agree more.

It had been pretty easy to get the rumours started. On the first day of the independent study unit, after the usual introduction to research methods and reminder of library etiquette, Mr. Rogman turned us loose in the library to start. We had to get our topics approved, which meant we had to do enough research to write a proposal first, and that was our window. We just needed to fake Trevor's research and frame him before the proposals were turned in. A few lunches in the library, and we had laid down more than enough of a false trail. The best part was that Trevor was actually forced to spend his lunches in the library, because his dad wanted him to study. He spent most of his time goofing off, but that didn't matter: he wouldn't have an alibi.

On Friday morning, an anonymous tip was turned in to the Athletic Association, claiming that Trevor Harrow had been researching how to use steroids on school computers. Elyse Ritsma, current president of the association, was Isobel's cousin, and she took the typed-out letter straight to our new principal, Mrs. Fiske. Mrs. Fiske promised to take action, beginning with an examination of Trevor's search history, and by then, no one could have stopped what was coming. Elyse liked her cousin a lot, and was understandably pissed at what Trevor had done to her. That anger, coupled with the tip that Trevor was cheating the exact same way he'd accused Isobel of, meant that Elyse had no qualms about coming out swinging.

By the end of the day, it was everywhere, as I learned when Adah got into the car. Elyse was always efficient, and no one felt like she was being mean, because everyone knew why she was mad at Trevor. Nothing was sure, of course, because the internet searches were circumstantial. There was no way to confirm if Trevor was clean or not without a drug test, which was going to take time to do. A week later, and Trevor sat by himself in the cafeteria, shoulders hunched over to make himself look shorter. He was an instant pariah, and even when the test eventually cleared him, everyone still thought he'd just got caught before he could execute his plan. No one believed that he would research two things at the same time. His reputation was used against him. He quit the volleyball team, which he'd been using to fill time until hockey season, and a second set of rumours sprung up about how he was going to drop out altogether. No one mentioned Isobel, but no one had to. I knew what we'd done, and that was enough.

Mrs. Fiske made us sit through an hour-long assembly about the school's zero-tolerance bullying policy, which had literally never been used to protect a kid from bullies. We sat on the floor of the gym and pretended to pay attention, but all I really cared about was the number of heads I saw turn for a furtive look at Trevor Harrow, the fallen hero. It was very satisfying.

"Whose turn is it to make dinner?" Adah asked as I turned onto the street where the elementary school was.

"Dottie," I said. Adah grimaced. "Hey, we all went through phases."

"Yeah, but you and I didn't have TikTok," Adah said. Technically Dottie didn't, either, because she was only twelve, but that hadn't stopped her from subjecting us to several recipes she found there, watching over Char's shoulder.

"I'm glad one of us is experimental," Char said. "When I was twelve, my dinner was usually grilled cheese and tomato soup."

"I *like* grilled cheese and tomato soup," Adah said. We pulled into the looped driveway of the elementary school. Dottie was sitting by herself, since most kids who didn't take a bus had to walk home. Being driven was something of a status symbol, and Dottie was *extremely* proud of it. Also, she beat the bus home by half an hour, because we didn't make any stops.

"Do you need anything from the grocery store?" I asked as Dottie settled herself in the back seat with Adah.

"No, I'm good," Dottie said. "I wanted to make my own gnocchi, but we wouldn't eat until like midnight if I did that, so Mum just got me the premade stuff."

We left town and I sped up to eighty. Four cars passed me immediately, because no one drove slower than one hundred on this road, but I couldn't afford any surprise expenditures. I listened to my siblings bicker about dinner and cooking and how long it took. Char leaned up against the window, and I took my eyes off the road a couple of times to look at them.

"I really am fine," they said. "Elementary school was small and no one cared. Now there are more people, so there's more noise. It'll keep getting noisier, so at least this is good practice."

"This is not what you should be practicing." I gripped the steering wheel tightly, furious and with no place for it to go.

"I know." They sighed. "But it's better than the alternative."

I thought about all the hand-me-downs Char had had to wear ever since they came out, because those were the clothes we had. I thought of all the people who still misgendered them because they were lazy or just didn't care enough to pay attention. I wanted to fight all their battles for them, because they shouldn't have had battles to begin with, but at the same time, I knew that wasn't what they wanted from me.

Maybe that's why I'd decided to get revenge for Isobel, even though she would never know about it. She might find out it happened—Facebook was the great leveler—but she wouldn't know who. Char didn't need me, and Isobel didn't need me, either, but I needed to do *some*thing, and Trevor Harrow had pissed me off. Was it nice? No. Was it ethical? Absolutely not. Was it good? Not even in the same ballpark.

But it was justice, and suddenly it didn't seem so bad that Char was facing down ignorant science teachers and too many questions from new kids who hadn't seen them grow up. It wasn't a big difference, but it was a difference all the same. And, just like Maddie said, no one suspected a thing. No one even thought to suspect a thing. It seemed like it had just happened, an organic result of the awfulness of teenagers.

The good girls were going to get away with it.

Again.

10.

Jenny Hoernig

Trevor Harrow stopped coming to school the week before Thanksgiving. I doubt he did it on purpose, but his timing was excellent. It was Commencement weekend in addition to the holiday, and Isobel was supposedly coming home for it. Poor grades notwithstanding, Trevor had technically graduated as well, and was expected to show up, along with his father. It didn't take all the heat off of Isobel, but it did give the gossips more targets.

I had been to Commencement every year since grade nine, because the band always played at it. Usually it was pretty boring, and Mrs. Heskie made us all get off the stage so we didn't cause a distraction by chatting. This year, I was not the only person hoping that she'd forget and let us stay through the whole thing.

"Oh my God, you will not *believe* the program," Louise announced, gracefully sinking down to sit cross-legged on the floor by Mags's locker. There were only fifteen minutes of lunch time left, so she was eating carrots while she spoke, which was always risky.

"Ugh, is it going to be long?" Jen asked. "These uniform bow ties have not gotten more comfortable."

"I have no idea," Louise said. She held a carrot in her mouth and brandished a salmon-pink paper. "Check out the awards list."

Every grade twelve advanced class had an award for the highest mark, a carryover from back when Ontario still had OACs. There were other awards for things like tech and non-sport extracurriculars, but the real money, literally, was in the subject awards.

"Holy shit," Maddie said.

I pulled the paper out of her hands and Mags read over my shoulder. Isobel Johnson had taken seven classes last year, and she'd won the subject award in six of them. She wasn't just getting a diploma tonight. This would cover almost her entire first year's tuition.

"She's going to have to go up onstage seven times," Mags said. "Well, maybe fewer, since some of the subjects are clumped together."

"I wouldn't want to do that under normal circumstances," Jen said. "I hate being in front of people." She paused. "They still have to give her the money if she doesn't come, right? Even if she changes her mind about coming at the last minute?"

"Yeah," I said. "They'll just mail her the cheques or something."

"I hope the Harrows sit where we can see them," Maddie said. "I want to see their faces every time Mrs. Kelly reads her name out."

The warning bell rang, and we went to our lockers for our afternoon books. None of us were really thinking about classes, though. Apparently, tonight was going to be quite the night.

For reasons lost to time, the setup for Commencement was not the same as a regular assembly. Instead of all the chairs facing the stage, they were arranged into angled wedges that faced the long side of the gym. The rarely used choir risers were hauled out from storage, and that's where the guests of honour sat, along with whatever teachers were in charge of running the show that year.

Behind them, hanging almost floor to ceiling, was a giant flag that was only brought out on special occasions. It had once flown on Parliament Hill, and Mr. Harrow had been ridiculously proud of it, even though literally anyone could apply to get one. I remember being alarmed to learn that the giant and presumably expensive Peace Tower flag was replaced every day, but usually I forgot it existed at all. Graduates would slide out of their rows, walk to the back via the middle aisle, and then come up one of the angled ones to receive their diplomas while we all found out if the administration had learned to pronounce everyone's names.

The band sat quietly while Mrs. Miller, who taught drafting and the occasional geography class, piped the graduates in. (I only knew what "Pomp and Circumstance" was because of television, because I'd never played it.) The instant the bagpipes disengaged, Mrs. Heskie cued us for the national anthem, and we watched all the parents scramble to their feet. Mr. Harrow had given his usual long-winded welcome for the last time when I was in grade nine, because after hearing it once, Mrs. Heskie cut him off every subsequent time. He was only here as a parent this year, but apparently Mrs. Heskie wasn't taking any chances with Mrs. Fiske, either.

Once everyone was seated again, the ceremony began. It was fairly standard: speeches, attempts at humour, itchy borrowed robes. At last we got to the names, and the grads made their way across the stage one by one to collect their diplomas.

"Isobel Johnson, daughter of William and Maisie Johnson, is attending Georgian College, studying early childhood education," Mrs. Kelly read.

Isobel had cut her hair, but otherwise there was no mistaking her. She accepted her diploma and went back to the marshalling area because if she sat down, she'd have to crawl over everyone to get her awards. Trevor Harrow, who had been separated from her by Alyson Hubert and Charlie Jefferson, was already back in his seat. Isobel didn't look at him.

My attention snapped back to the line of graduates, and I watched Isobel march to the front. She didn't look entirely comfortable, but she was there, and that was what really mattered.

According to Maddie's wishes, the Harrows had, in fact, sat so that we could see their faces. We watched while Mrs. Harrow's lips disappeared and Mr. Harrow's face turned redder and redder as he scowled. By the sixth announcement, I thought they might actually get up and leave, but they were seated in the middle of a row, so they'd have to make a scene if they wanted to get out.

"That was beautiful," Maddie said, bumping the back of my shoulder to get my attention. She'd left her spot to come sit closer to me and Jen, but she returned now as the closing remarks began.

Mrs. Heskie cued us for the recessional march, and I made myself focus for just a few more minutes while we played. She dismissed us as soon as it was done, and I all but ran back to the music room.

I went through the motions of putting away my saxophone on autopilot. Somehow I was going to have to pull myself together and drive to Maddie's house, but right now, I felt like I could curl up in the tuba case if they'd let me. It was like all the emotional stress of what we'd done to Trevor Harrow caught up with me at once. Being the one who'd made the wish felt heavy. No one had cared that he was gone. It was like we'd erased him from the social landscape he used to control. It was kind of an amazing feeling, to be honest, and I wasn't ashamed to be having it.

"Come on." I linked arms with Maddie and we headed towards

the door of the music room. Jen was two seconds behind us, and by the time we got to the parking lot, she had linked arms, too.

The mid-October night was crisp, but not yet cold. It was going to be the kind of Thanksgiving where you could go outside, which was always nicer than one with gross fall weather. Or worse: snow. Jen got in the back seat of my car and pushed my overnight bag out of her way. She knocked it over, and since I hadn't zipped it shut, the shirt I had packed for tomorrow fell out.

"Sorry," she said.

"No worries," I told her. "Just shove it back in."

Jen folded my shirt and put it back in the bag. She always took good care of clothes, even when they weren't hers.

"I like this one," she said. "It's a good colour for you."

"My mum is a champion thrifter," I said, and it was true. I didn't talk about it much, but the only reason I was remotely in style was that Mum treated thrifting as a second job. Sometimes, she made more money reselling online than she did at the photography store.

"Yeah," Jen said, a bit absently.

Maddie turned the radio up, even though it was only like two minutes to her house from the school. I didn't want to talk to Jen about clothes, so I didn't complain. Usually I have a strict "driver picks the music" rule, but I was happy for the distraction. The local radio station piped in Ryan Seacrest in the evenings because it was cheaper than hiring someone, and on Fridays, that meant American Top 40.

We dropped Jen off at the foot of her driveway, and then I pulled in behind Maddie's dad and parked. We sat there, listening to the last bit of the song.

"Well," said Maddie, "that's two."

"Yeah," I said. "Any regrets?"

She thought about it for a minute.

"No," she said. "This one was way more personal, like, an attack on a person instead of a building, so it feels different, but I don't feel bad about the result."

"Neither do I," I said.

"You don't sound like you don't have regrets," Maddie said. "What's wrong?"

"It's not a regret," I said. "More like a 'there but for the grace of God.' Someone could do something like this to Char, and I wouldn't be able to stop it."

"I thought they were okay?" Maddie said. It was clearly not a possibility that had occurred to her.

"They are," I said. "I just worry. They watched the volleyball team fall apart last year, too, and they know about Isobel because Isobel told them as, like, a solidarity thing."

"That's so sweet," Maddie said. She was quiet for a moment, and then she continued, "I don't think about leaving town very often. I assume I will, I just don't dwell on it, but there's going to be so much out there for Char."

It kills me that I can't make a completely safe home for them here. But I have helped make this town better. And something tells me we're only just getting started.

"Yeah," I said. "I know."

THIRD WISH:

Utterance

(OR: MAGS SHARPE'S 17TH BIRTHDAY)

11.
Mags Sharpe

I don't think any of us really expected Jenny's wish to go so quickly. Even though we had to wait for a bit to get started, the actual rumour-spreading part went like wildfire, and a short time later, Trevor was gone. The grass had taken longer than that to die, and it had definitely taken longer than that for someone at the church to notice what was happening to the ground. That felt a little bit more controlled. If the Trevor thing had gotten away from us, it could have gone very badly.

I'm smart enough to admit that part of the reason is that I had pretty much full control over killing the grass. I went into that supply room every week and salted the bottles myself. I had been part of the planning for Trevor's thing, sure, but in the end all it had taken was Maddie cocking her head at the right person. It was explosive and dangerous and powerful.

And I definitely kind of liked it.

I spent Thanksgiving weekend at home. My brothers and sisters spent most of their time outside, because there were no dishes to wash out there, but I had cracked the code on dishwashing a while ago. Dad would wash pretty much any dish that Mum used, so the key was to bake while she was cooking, and Dad would take care of it. Add in Uncle David trying to "help out" his way back into his sister's good graces, and Dad might not have to wash any dishes, either.

We were expecting the Sharpe cousins on Sunday for dinner. There weren't any Shropshall cousins—first cousins, anyway—which always made me sad when I was a kid. Everyone else I knew had cousins on both sides, even if it was only two or three. One might argue that eight Sharpes and three Shropshalls was its own party, but since all but one of them lived on the same property, it wasn't the same.

All but two of them, I mean.

For their parts, Mum and Grandma made sure that they didn't accidentally make a caretaker out of me. It happened anyway, but they made sure not to let David and Colin out of household chores just because they'd been in the barn and that sort of thing. It would never be equal, and I didn't think it could be, but the important thing was that everyone was trying. Even Uncle David, though his attempts at gender parity were usually a bit patronizing. Moving around the kitchen, carefully staying out of Mum's way while delivering dirty dishes to the sink, he looked almost like he belonged here.

I had been avoiding him. I hadn't been to church since the beginning of school, and his parishioners had definitely noticed. We were already noticeable because we went to public schools, but me skipping mass was a whole new level, and not just because there was no one to replace me in youth group, so now the grown-ups had to do it. Spending the summer with Jenny was eye-opening in more than one way. I saw the hurt in her expression every time someone said how nice it was to see her again and during the long pause while everyone tried to complete the question "And how are your . . ." without saying "sisters." I didn't want to be part of that. But I didn't know how to stop, either.

Because here's the thing: I do believe in God. I had a growing number of doubts about several institutions established in His name, but the God part was natural for me. It was a comfort when I needed it and a challenge when I got too comfortable.

It's mostly been a challenge lately.

"Mags, have you seen my . . ." Colin burst into the kitchen, looking for his sunglasses. He'd got them three weeks ago for his birthday, and if there was the *slightest* bit of sunlight, he insisted on wearing them. Of course, he was also twelve, so he lost them on the regular.

"I put them in your shoe basket," I told him. "But that was after I almost sat on them, so please stop leaving them on the couch."

"I don't want them to smell like shoes," Colin protested. "They go on my nose."

"You're tall enough to reach the key shelf," I pointed out. "Put them up there. Bonus points: Teddy won't be able to steal them."

Teddy could probably climb up a wall of ice, but everyone needed to feel secure about their belongings sometimes.

"Thanks, Mags!" Colin shouted, already halfway out the door, which he slammed behind him.

"Mags, if you want to go outside, we can manage," Mum said. Dinner was in half an hour—in theory—so everything was done and under a hot lamp, except for the turkey, which was still settling.

"Thanks, but I'm good," I said. I had been icing turkey-shaped cookies for what felt like hours, but it was time for beaks and wattles, so they were finally looking nice.

"She can't be outside playing when the Jantzis get here," Dad teased.

"We all know Aaron is going straight up whatever tree Teddy has newly discovered, and neither of them are coming down until we tell them we'll start eating without them," Grandma said. Everyone was laughing except for Uncle David now.

"I'm like ten minutes from being done," I said. "And then I'm going to go with Grandma to get Grandpa from town."

"They look really good, Mags," Uncle David said. "I will feel slightly bad before I bite one in half."

"That's more than anyone else," I said. I smiled at him, and the relief in his eyes almost killed me where I stood.

I looked away and got the red buttercream ready in the piping bag. I was using butterscotch chips for the beaks, and they all needed a tiny bit of icing to stick, and then I'd make the red line of the wattle. Clara didn't like eating things with eyes, so four of the turkeys did not have faces. Exactly ten minutes later, I put the icing bag down and set the last cookie on the plate.

"I'll take them to the cold room," Uncle David said.

I knew he wouldn't drop them, but it was still nerve-racking to watch someone else handle them when I had done so much work. I deliberately turned away and went into the powder room off the kitchen to clean up.

When I got back, Grandma had her keys and was ready to go. I put on my shoes and jacket, and followed her to the car. She didn't really need me, but I tried not to let her go to the nursing home alone any more than I absolutely had to. If I could drive, I could have picked Grandpa up myself. Not getting my license was selfish, but I couldn't bring myself to book the test. Mum and Dad never asked about it, either, which was nice of them.

It was only a few minutes to drive into town, but when we got to the nursing home, Grandpa wasn't ready for us yet.

"I'm so sorry," the nurse's aide said. "We had to give him prune juice at lunch, and we didn't want to get him dressed until, you know, after."

"It's all right, dear," Grandma said. She knew all their names, but this one was relatively new. "I was here yesterday, and I knew they were going to have to take steps today."

"Anyway, I'll get him dressed in the bathroom, and you two can wait here," the aide said.

"Oh, you go," Grandma said, stopping outside the door to Grandpa's room. "I know you're busy, and it's nothing I haven't seen before."

Grandma didn't usually help out, but the nurses, PSWs, and aides were always slammed, so if we were in a hurry, she would step in. Grandma went straight into the bathroom, and I went to sit in the empty chair. Mr. Hastings was here, sitting in his wheelchair and looking out the window. Unlike Grandpa, his memory is fine. He had a stroke a few years ago, and did not recover full mobility, but his mind is as sharp as it ever was.

"Hello, Mags," he said. He slurs his words a little bit, but he works with a speech pathologist, and Dahlia walks over to read with him on Saturdays. "How are you doing?"

"I'm very well, thank you," I said. "Is Dahlia coming?"

"She's been and gone," he told me. "They're springing me tomorrow for the day. Are you sure you're okay? You look like you're thinking too much."

Mr. Hastings had always been like that, but it never got less unnerving. Still, he wasn't a family member or one of my friends, and God knows, I needed to talk to someone outside my bubble.

"Mr. Hastings, do you believe in God?" I asked. I mean, I knew he read the Torah and observed the holy days as much as he could, but Dahlia said that sometimes being Jewish is as much culture as it is religion. I'd definitely felt that way about Catholicism lately, and even though I knew it wasn't the same thing, it was starting to smother me.

"Yes," said Mr. Hastings without a moment's hesitation. "Probably because we're allowed to have a lot more arguments with Him than you are."

His left eye was always half-closed, but there was no mistaking the wink he gave me. I laughed in spite of myself.

"I used to worry about my grandkids," Mr. Hastings said. "They were always the only ones in class that weren't having Christmas, or eating hot dogs without asking questions first, or needing an exemption because someone scheduled a test on Yom Kippur again. I thought it would either make them fanatics or completely uninterested. But they turned out okay. And that's why I believe in God. Does that help?"

"Not really," I said. "But also kind of yes?"

"Then my work here is done." Mr. Hastings grinned. "Say hello to young Aaron for me."

He winked again, this time even more obviously, and I turned pink. Before I could answer, Grandma opened the bathroom door and led Grandpa out. I got up quickly. It was always easier to keep him moving once you got him started.

"Bye, Peter," Grandma called, and Mr. Hastings raised his right hand to wave.

I took Grandpa's arm and led him towards the door. He hadn't recognized either of us yet, but he always seemed better on the farm. It hurt, because he couldn't live there anymore, but that was why we brought him home when we could.

Sure enough, he didn't say anything until we pulled in the driveway. Then his eyes lit up and he leaned forwards.

"I know this house!" he said. Then he smiled, and I thought I might almost understand what Mr. Hastings meant about believing in God.

12.
Mags Sharpe

The Jantzis' minivan was parked in the driveway when we got home. I could see Aaron's shoes hanging down out of the pine tree near the drive shed. It had higher branches than Teddy's usual favourites, so I knew he was taking advantage of having help. Grandma had Grandpa by the arm, and after I made sure they were both okay, I headed for the tree.

"No girls allowed!" shouted Teddy as soon as I came into sight. I couldn't really blame him. David and Colin ignored him, and he's three years younger than Clara, so he was subjected to all manner of exclusions.

"Hey," said Aaron, grinning at me, "how about we make an exception?"

"No exceptions!" Teddy insisted. I wasn't entirely sure he knew what the word meant. "Unless she brought cookies."

"The cookies are inside, Frederick," I told him.

"I'm a bear," he growled. "I'm a Teddy."

"Mum is going to call you 'Frederick' if you don't come down and wash your hands," I said. "And you know what that means."

Teddy was desperately trying to get his bedtime moved back to eight, with variable success. Tonight was especially important, because our company wouldn't leave until late, and Teddy didn't want to miss a single second of it, unless Clara had to as well.

"Fine," he said. "Catch me!"

I had about half a second to get my hands up before I took a five-year-old to the chest. He knocked the wind out of me, but I managed to stay on my feet. Teddy was laughing hysterically, and hugged me tightly before squirming enough that I set him down.

"No kissing until I'm gone," he yelled over his shoulder. "No one wants to see that."

"No one is going to," I yelled back at him. One thing I liked about Aaron was that he respected my severe dislike of PDA.

"Hi," Aaron said. His exit from the tree was much more digni-fied, and when he held out his hand, I took it.

"Hi," I said. "Sorry I'm late. The nursing home isn't exactly predictable."

"We've only been here a few minutes," Aaron said. "Ted just works fast, that's all. How's your granddad doing?"

"I think he'll be okay," I said. "Tomorrow, when the cousins are here, it'll be a lot noisier, and that's usually harder for him, but tonight there's only five extras. For us that's hardly anything."

The Jantzis started joining us for dinner on Thanksgiving Saturday a few years ago. My mum and Julie are close, especially since Grandpa moved into the nursing home where Julie works when she's not at the hospital, Louise and I have been best friends since we were babies, and Aaron works here. When Aaron and I started dating two years ago, nothing really changed. We just talked more, and occasionally we made out a little bit if no one else was around. When there are sixteen people at the dinner table, that can be a challenge.

We held hands all the way across the yard, and then he opened the door for me. It was like walking into a wall of sound, but in all the good and familiar ways. We kicked off our shoes and headed into the dining room. A kids' table would have been pointless, so everyone squeezed around the giant oak table my grandpa had bought forty years ago. It had three leaves in the middle, and Dad had added two card tables to the end, and that let everyone fit. We put Grandpa at the foot so that Mum or Julie could help him eat. (There was an argument over that every year, which boiled down to: Mum and Grandma and Julie each thought the others deserved time off, Dad had to make sure Clara and Elsie didn't kill each other, I shirked because boundaries are important, and Uncle David pretended it wasn't his problem. This year, it looked like Julie had won, and she was helping Grandpa get his serviette and cutlery settled.)

We each claimed a place and drinks were poured, and then Grandma said grace because she was better at it than Uncle David was, and even he would admit it. Then Paul Jantzi and David tried to race each other to the front of the line in the kitchen and got booted to the end while Grandma went first and Dad fixed plates for Julie and Grandpa. Finally the grown-ups were finished, and the kids pushed and shoved their way through. Louise and I were near the front, and when we got back to the table, Louise calmly switched her cranberry juice with Aaron's apple cider so that we could sit beside each other and Aaron was moved down between Clara and Colin. They played that game a lot, and it was entirely in good fun. When Aaron got back, he pretended to kick up a fuss, and then all the adults teased him, and everyone was laughing.

There were so many conversations going on that it was hard to follow anything but the person you were talking to. It didn't take me very long to notice that no one was talking to Uncle David. He was sitting across from Julie, and since Grandpa didn't recognize him right now, the only person he had to talk with was Elsie, who was carefully keeping her turkey gravy separate from her potato gravy, and extracting all the onions from her stuffing.

I tried not to let it bother me. His happiness was not my responsibility. But I couldn't help feeling like it was my fault, because it kind of was.

"Crap, I forgot to put the second tray of stuffing into the chafing dish," Mum said. She started to get up, but I stopped her.

"I'll get it," I said. "I have to take the ice cream cake out of the freezer anyway, or we'll never be able to cut it."

"I'll help," said Uncle David, also getting to his feet.

I blinked at him, but couldn't think of a good reason to refuse, so I just turned and walked into the kitchen. He followed me, but didn't say anything while I put on the oven mitts.

"The cake is in the little freezer," I said, pointing towards the door that led to the cold room.

"Right," he said, and went to get it.

By the time he got back, I had half the dressing into the chafing dish. I needed a candle, but before I could ask him to get one, he set the cake down on the dry sink and leaned back on his hands. I had been watching him psych himself up to give speeches for my entire life, so I knew he had something to say.

"How are you doing?" he asked eventually. "School and stuff, I mean."

"Fine," I said. "It's busy, obviously, but it's all good."

"How is Aaron?" he asked.

"Also fine," I said. "This is the first time I've talked to him in a few days, and we haven't had much catch-up time."

"You know I used to worry about you two," Uncle David said. "Especially after he went to Ridgetown."

"Did you think we'd break up?" I asked. I certainly had. What made perfect sense in the little world of my parents' farm was harder to explain in the real world. But Aaron hadn't changed his mind about anything, and neither had I, so it was working out.

"Oh, I knew you wouldn't," Uncle David said. "It's just that the whole thing with Amelia Chaser opened my eyes to what was going on in my family and in the community."

I froze, fury burning cold. He must have sensed it, because he actually took a step away from me.

"Are you talking as my priest or as my uncle?" I asked.

"Which one is your mum less likely to kill when she finds out?" he asked, nervously twisting his fingers.

"Uncle," I hissed.

"Okay, then." He took a moment to gather his thoughts. "I just want you to be safe. I feel like you're drifting away from me, Mags. You used to think church was fun."

This man did not suspect that I had drifted into his office to desecrate holy water this year. He didn't even think to suspect.

"Do you know the moment it stopped being fun?" I asked.

"No," he said.

"When I was in grade five, I realized that I was allowed to help decorate the altar, I was allowed to wash linens for the altar, and I was allowed to clean the altar, but I wasn't allowed to serve at the altar on Sunday mornings." He started to protest, but I cut him off. "The *second* worst part of that is that the altar rules were only changed in 1992. The *worst* part is that it's up to the bishop to make the change, and none of ours have ever cared enough to formally amend the rules for our parish."

"Mags, you could have spearheaded something," he said. "You literally know a guy."

"I thought about it," I admitted. "But it sucks to have to ask for something you should have—and should have *always* had."

"I'm sorry, Mags," he said. I believed him. But I didn't care.

"You were so excited when David was old enough to be an altar boy," I said. I was twisting the knife now, but he deserved it. "You gave him a gift card for books and told him how thrilled you were to finally have someone to carry on the family tradition. And I knew that no matter what you did or said, and no matter what I did or said, you would always believe that God thinks David can do things I can't solely because he has a penis."

Mum appeared in the kitchen door, the smile falling off her face as she realized what she was walking into. I finished spooning the stuffing into the dish and got the candle myself.

"I'm sorry, Mags," he repeated. He sounded like he'd aged ten years, and I refused to let myself feel bad about it.

"I know you are," I told him. "It doesn't help."

He turned without a word, and my mum made space for him to return to the dining room. I felt like the ground had opened up and I was falling. I hadn't meant to say all that, but I felt so good now that I had. I was almost lightheaded.

"Mags, are you okay?" Mum came over with the lighter and lit the wick under the dish.

"Yeah," I said. "I might not be Catholic anymore."

"We'll work it out," she said. "Assuming you want to."

"I do," I said. God was still important. "I mean, Aaron's Anglican—"

"Mags," Mum said, her hand over her heart like she was about to keel over. "I beg you"—her lips turned up in a smile—"on behalf of your Scottish ancestors, at least *try* Presbyterianism first."

I laughed, and it was like a weight had lifted off of everything. I grabbed another dinner roll and headed back into the dining room. When I sat down, Louise took my hand under the table and I squeezed.

"Are you okay?" she whispered. Aaron was looking at me, too, so I smiled even though he couldn't hear us.

"Yeah," I said. "I think I've decided on my wish."

13.
Mags Sharpe

On the surface, my wish was pretty close to Jenny's. There was a girl who was hurting and a boy who needed to pay. But unlike Jenny, I wasn't limiting my target to one boy. I was going after a whole group of them.

Elizabeth Stewart was a year younger than we were, in grade eleven. She was kind of friends with Jenny's sister Adah, but only because Adah was friends with everyone. As far as I knew, Elizabeth didn't have anyone close to her. She just hung out in Adah's orbit, and being in orbit was being at risk.

Elizabeth's parents were in the process of getting a divorce. They'd had a messy, public fight at the athletic banquet last June, and by the end of the summer, they'd decided it was over. Mr. Stewart moved into the apartment over Jenny's mum's photography store because the Stewarts owned the building.

Years ago, during a sleepover at Jenny's house, she'd told us that her mother developed racy photos all the time. Jenny's mum had started working at the store when she was in high school and eventually bought the business when the owners retired. Before digital cameras were everywhere, people would bring rolls of film, apparently not considering the part where Jenny's mum was going to see the pictures, too. The work brought her fun mysteries as well, like a roll of film someone found in the attic that turned out to be their parents' engagement photos, but most of the really juicy stories were, well, juicy.

The store was also one of the few in town that carried lots of small, very expensive, and easily stolen merchandise, and after a near miss with some thieves a couple years ago, Jenny's mother had ordered security cameras. The Stewarts had given their permission, since it was their building.

I had been in the shop in September, looking at the old photography equipment. When he was younger, Grandpa had liked taking pictures, but no one seemed to know where his camera was. Grandma did have a picture of him in his early thirties with his own camera around his neck. I thought that if I got him a camera he recognized, he might be able to try. His nurses thought it was good idea, and I went to Jenny's mum's to go shopping.

The vintage camera "section" was really a glorified storage closet at the back corner of the store, and it wasn't very well organized, but when I showed Mrs. Hoernig the picture of Grandpa's camera, she said she thought she had one. "Head on back. I need to finish something at the counter first, and then I'll help you find it." I walked into the closet just as Mr. Stewart burst through the front door, too worked up to consider that there might be a customer in the store.

"I need to look at the security tapes," he demanded. "There's . . . there's something on last night's tape I don't want Elizabeth to see. My wife doesn't need to know, either, but I don't want Elizabeth to see it. This whole . . . thing has upset her enough, and I don't want to make her feel worse."

There was no reason for Elizabeth to see the security tapes ever, and that thin excuse raised every suspicion Mrs. Hoernig could have had. She said she couldn't show him the recordings right this instant, but she'd email them after she closed. Mr. Stewart then demanded that she simply destroy the "tapes" immediately, and when Mrs. Hoernig calmly explained she couldn't delete the digital files—that were stored on an external server—while the store was open, he got angry and stomped out, saying he'd expect the email that night.

I waited about five minutes before coming up to the counter with the camera I'd found. Mrs. Hoernig looked up from her computer screen, surprised to see me.

"Oh, fuck," she said. "I forgot you were here."

"I can keep a secret," I told her.

"Mags, if this turns into a legal debacle . . ." She trailed off. "I'm sorry I didn't cut him off. I was so thrown off by everything he was demanding."

"It's okay."

"I just emailed last night's recordings, and I cc'd his wife," she told me. "She can decide about Elizabeth, but there's no way I'm keeping information from her if she can use it in the divorce. And she co-owns the building. She has just as much right to see them as he does."

"I definitely don't mind helping with that," I said. "I saw the fight at the banquet, and it was pretty bad."

"You and everyone else." Mrs. Hoernig sighed. "This town puts everyone in everyone's business. Did you decide on a camera?"

I paid her and left, and I didn't really think about the Elizabeth situation again until Thanksgiving. I never had any reason to think about it because Mrs. Stewart hadn't shown Elizabeth the tape of her father bringing a college-aged girl from three towns over up to his apartment. Mrs. Stewart hadn't told anyone besides my dad, either. I knew she was using it in her divorce filings because she was one of the Sharpe cousins, and she'd filled out the paperwork at our kitchen table because she didn't want to do it by herself. Small town, everyone's business. I was peeling carrots at the time, and no one even thought to ask me to leave the room.

Everyone at school knew that Elizabeth's parents were getting divorced, but no one besides me knew exactly why. There were dozens of rumours, but the one that stuck was the one that said Elizabeth's dad was leaving because he couldn't handle Elizabeth doing drugs. As far as anyone could prove, Elizabeth had only ever smoked pot at parties, like half the student population, but that didn't matter. The rumour spread faster than when we took down Trevor. The stress made Elizabeth start pulling out her hair. She bit all her fingernails down so that sometimes the cuticles bled when she held a pen. She lost weight. She looked terrible. And then everyone said it was probably the heroin.

ECSS had three floors and several stairwells. The school had been built in stages, so the bottom was a giant square with a few protrusions for things like the music room and the little gym, the second floor was L-shaped, and the third floor was a straight line. The main stairwell was also the oldest, and went up all the way. It had the highest traffic, but because of a quirk of construction, it also had a weird niche thing between the first and second flight. That's where the boys hung out.

They'd been there for years. It was a weird conglomeration of friend groups as the spot was handed down across student generations. They hassled girls about literally everything, but mostly went in for verbal sexual harassment. Every once in a while, a teacher caught them, and they all got in trouble. But it was only ever a lull. Within two weeks, they'd be right back at it. Since the teachers weren't going to solve the problem, the students took matters into their own hands: we just used another stairwell, even if it meant a detour.

It got to be so habit-forming that one time in grade eleven, Maddie actually did it while walking with a teacher. Mrs. Bowles, who mostly taught English, had asked her where she was going, and seeing an opportunity, Maddie immediately narked. The boys got in trouble, and we had two weeks of blessed relief, but then they were right back at it, and we were taking the long way around.

Every once in a while, someone would be in a hurry or they'd forget that the universe was cruel, and they'd take the main stairs. If you were in a group, it usually wasn't so bad, but Elizabeth was frequently on her own, or at least walking on the edge of whatever group of girls she was with. In other words, the perfect target.

"Hey, Liz, you're gonna start losing your boobs if you keep losing weight, and then no one will ever want to fuck you" was how it started, and it only got worse. Soon there were rumours about self-harm in addition to everything else, that Elizabeth's heroin tracks were being cut up by her own razor blade, and she was going to have to find another drug of choice if she kept it up, because soon she wouldn't have anywhere to put the needle.

All through October it got worse and worse. Adah punched one of the boys one day and got an in-school suspension for it because she broke his nose. No one cared why she'd done it—except every girl in the building, who treated her like a hero. And still, Elizabeth shrank further in on herself. I felt like my mid-November birthday was never going to get here.

When the day finally arrived, the party was at my house. Grandma let us use her kitchen while she spent the afternoon with my siblings. We made cookies, which is to say that Louise restrained herself from critiquing our baking techniques, and that there were a few cookies left over by the time we'd stopped eating cookie dough, and ordered pizza. There might have been a movie, but the truth was that everyone was excited to hear my wish, and I was ready to tell them.

"I want to hurt the boys who are hurting Elizabeth Stewart," I said.

"There's like fifteen of them," Jenny said. "As much as I want to punch them all, I don't think that's reasonable."

"Hurt them emotionally," I clarified.

"I am not sure if they have emotions," Louise said. Her face was curled up in distaste.

"Dahlia said Elizabeth dropped off the basketball team," Jen said. "And she didn't go back to the badminton team when it started up, either."

"You talk to Dahlia now?" Maddie asked.

"Shut up," Jen said. "Don't get distracted."

It was a nice distraction, but we had work to do, so I just grinned and kept going.

"We're going to get them caught doing something awful," I said.

"That never works," Jenny said. "They get caught like four times a semester."

"I know," I said. "That's why we need to plan it out. Because I want them to get caught doing something awful to me."

"Why would that make a difference?" Jen asked.

I smiled grimly. If there was going to be Catholic guilt, then I was damn sure going to take advantage of it. It seemed more than fair.

"Because this time, they're going to get caught by someone the administration can't just placate and ignore," I told them. "This time, they're going to get caught by Uncle David."

14.
Mags Sharpe

I thought the hard part was going to be getting a Catholic priest to come visit a non-Catholic public high school, but it took care of itself (or Someone Else made sure . . . it really depends on how you want to look at it). That meant I was stuck with the other hard part: actually taking the stairs and subjecting myself to the boys, so that if we ever got my uncle within earshot, he'd be hearing material they'd practiced at. It helped that the other girls took turns coming with me—except Jen, who was exempt because boys had been making fun of her chest since grade six.

Then two Sundays after my birthday, Uncle David came over for dinner. Family dinners had more or less returned to normal, even if any conversation he and I had was a little bit strained, and Mum stared daggers at him if she thought he was prying. I was glad, not because I was in a hurry to repair our relationship, but because the younger kids were still figuring themselves out, and I wanted them to be able to make informed decisions.

Anyway, we were just digging into Elsie's fourth attempt at pie (attempts one through three had gone straight out to the barn and the piglet she was raising for 4-H), when David looked up from shoveling food into his face.

"Uncle David, do you still have those like billion pictures you took when you went to Jordan that time?"

"I don't think it was a billion pictures, but yes," Uncle David said.

"Do you think you could pick like twenty of the really good ones and come into my history class?" he asked. "We're doing ancient history right now, and all of Mr. Attis's slides are old and blurry."

I tried not to hold my breath as everything fell directly into my lap. It was week two, so David had history after lunch. If Uncle David came early, we'd be able to set something up. The central staircase was the logical one for him to take.

"That sounds like fun," Uncle David said. "What day? I have some meetings this week, but we can make time."

"Probably Friday," David said. "Will that work?"

"Absolutely," Uncle David told him. "I left my work phone at home, but I'll update my calendar when I get back to it."

"It's going to be an uncle thing, right?" David asked, remembering to clarify.

"Yes." Uncle David smiled. He looked down the table at me, but I pretended I didn't see him. "It's an uncle thing."

"Cool," David said. "I'll text you after my teacher tells me it's okay."

And that would have been that, except it got even better. On Wednesdays, Uncle David had a standing lunch meetup with the Anglican and United Church ministers at one of the local coffee shops. They'd only been kicked out twice for raising their voices at each other, and only then because Agnes—the owner—thought they should be exemplars of dignity. In any case, the Anglican minister had also been to Jordan, and her pictures were even newer than Uncle David's, so she volunteered to come, too.

"I hope this works," Jenny said. We were waiting by the water fountain on the second floor. "We're not going to be able to set up a second run."

"Have a little faith," I told her. She rolled her eyes. I didn't hold it against her.

"Reverend Alden!" we heard Louise call out from the bottom of the stairs. We couldn't hear what followed, but I knew she was asking a question about Advent services, because that was the plan. Half a second later my phone buzzed. Jenny saluted, and I headed for the stairs.

As I walked down the first flight, the boys caught sight of me and started to catcall. They'd given up on "clever" insults relating to my name, but I hoped they enunciated. I kept my chin up, hugging my books tight and not looking at any of them. At the bottom of the first flight, I had to walk past their niche and then turn to keep going down. I could see the back of both the adults' heads as they listened to Louise, and David standing awkwardly beside them, waiting to escort them up to his classroom.

"Hey, Mags, how's your boyfriend?" Uncle David definitely heard my name. I saw him straighten up, though he was still looking at Louise. I took the stairs very, very slowly.

"Come over here and let me show you a few things." I knew if I turned around, he'd have his hands in his pockets. I didn't. "I'm sure Aaron's learning all kinds of stuff about farming. You wouldn't want to fall behind."

The taunts didn't even make sense, but somehow they still made my skin crawl.

"Maybe she likes it behind."

I froze. I forgot the plan. I was going to turn around and punch him myself.

But I didn't have to.

Uncle David *and* Reverend Alden came charging up the stairs towards me. The boys, who were laughing at each other's wittiness, shut up *real* fast when confronted with not one, but two clerical collars. Louise came up the stairs and reached out to put her hands on my shoulders.

"How dare you?!" Reverend Alden yelled.

Mrs. Bowles appeared at the top of the stairwell. Jenny was behind her, eyes wide, but she didn't come down.

"What's going on here?" Mrs. Bowles asked.

"Were you aware that these boys were harassing my niece?" Uncle David asked.

"Oh, it's not just Mags." Dahlia Hastings had come up from nowhere and stood beside Louise. "They have something special for all of us. For me it's usually something 'clever' about pigs."

"Office," barked Mrs. Bowles. "All of you, right now."

She herded all eight boys down the stairs. Even momentarily cowed, it was a big job for one person.

"David, could you tell your history teacher we'll be along?" Reverend Alden said. "We're going to go help. Mags will bring us up afterwards, right, Mags?"

"Uh, sure," I said. "I mean, yes. I can do that."

"Great," said Uncle David. "Dahlia, right? One of the Hastings girls? Could you come, too?"

"Of course," Dahlia said, and linked arms with me. Louise ran up the stairs to stop Jenny from crashing the party, and to go meet up with Maddie and Jen. We followed Mrs. Bowles to the office.

We had to meet in the guidance office, because there wasn't enough room in the principal's. Mrs. Fiske listened while Reverend Alden outlined what she and Uncle David had overheard.

"I'm very sorry," Mrs. Fiske said. She turned to me and Dahlia. "I know this has been an ongoing problem."

"How ongoing?" Uncle David asked.

"This is my first year here—"

"At least since grade nine," Dahlia interrupted. "The boys just keep spawning whenever some of them graduate."

"I know that bullying is hard to counteract," Uncle David began, "but surely something can be done?"

Mrs. Fiske looked at me and Dahlia again.

"I can start with in-school suspension," she said. "That means they'll be out of their classrooms. Probably in the library study room because there are so many of them. They'll have to do all their regular classwork, plus whatever essays I choose to assign."

"That's a good start," Uncle David said. He thought for a minute. "You know, I can't free up every lunch hour, but I bet Reverend Alden and I can up with one or two a week where we come in and lecture them about appropriate behaviour."

"Absolutely," Reverend Alden said. "We'll do it together, for as many months as you like, and if their parents want to attend as well, they are more than welcome."

I fought to keep a triumphant smile off of my face.

Two of the boys winced. The rest just looked angry and defeated. I could not believe how well this had turned out. We didn't catch all of them, but hopefully once word got around about how severely the eight we had caught were being dealt with, the rest of them would shut up for a good while. The boy who frequently asked Dahlia about the pig had been the one to come up with the especially vile things said to Elizabeth, so nabbing him was extra good. High school permanent records weren't that applicable to real life, but it would hang over all of them for a while, at least.

"Oh," I said, remembering. Everyone looked at me. "And you should clear Adah Hoernig's record, too. While we're at it."

"What did Adah do?" Uncle David asked.

Dahlia laughed. "What do you think?"

"Good for her," said Reverend Alden, looking over her shoulder and seeing the boy with the nose splint and still slightly purple eyes.

The bell rang, and Mrs. Fiske went around behind the desk to write down everyone's names.

"Girls, you can go," she said. "I'll take Father Shropshall and Reverend Alden upstairs when we're done here. Boys, your in-school suspension starts now. Go and get everything out of your lockers you'll need for the afternoon, and if you aren't all in the library by the time I get there, I will add a week to your suspensions."

Dahlia and I made a quick exit and managed to not start laughing until we were halfway down the hall outside the office.

"Oh my God," I said.

"Right?" Dahlia said. "Usually I am not here for violations of the Geneva convention, but that was amazing. And right in front of *two* priests. Or a priest and a . . . Are Anglicans also priests?"

"Yes," I said.

"Amazing," she said. She stopped laughing and, after a thoughtful moment, turned to ask me a question. "Can you wait for me after school today?"

"Yeah," I said. "What do you need?"

"I just wanted to walk over to the nursing home with you, if that's okay," she said. "It doesn't make sense for us not to go together."

"Sure," I said. "I'll be at my locker."

"Awesome," she said, and we split ways to head to class.

Jenny and Maddie were waiting for me in biology, and we didn't have time to talk before the bell rang, but it was clear from my face how everything had gone down.

"Three for three," Jenny whispered.

Three for three.

15.
Mags Sharpe

It was a risk, but I couldn't resist it. That weekend, I went into the sewing shop in town, because Elizabeth worked there, and I was pretty sure she'd be alone. Like Julia Hoernig's photography store, the sewing shop had clung on by sheer will and special online orders. I brought Elsie in a few times over the summer. She'd gotten really into friendship bracelets and needed embroidery floss and beads. It gave her something to do when she visited Grandpa and he didn't know who she was.

It was a tiny space. The restaurant next door took up what used to be the back half. Internal architecture changed inside these old buildings sometimes, to meet the needs of the stores that remained. There was a fire door at the back, but the front door was used for deliveries. If Elizabeth needed the washroom, she had to flip the sign and use the restaurant bathrooms. The weird interdependencies to stay on Main Street.

The bell rang when I opened the door, but I couldn't see Elizabeth at first. The walls were stacked high with bolts of cloth, and the two small aisles were tall and crammed with everything from needles to cutting mats. It was like walking into a magical workshop, where everything was potential and none of the finished products existed yet, because imagination hadn't made them physical.

"Hi," said Elizabeth. I could tell by her expression that she had no idea why I might be in the store. Our parents were cousins, but we weren't that close.

"Hi," I said. "I know this is going to seem a bit weird, but are you okay?"

To be completely honest, she looked much better in the store than she did at school. The defensiveness was gone. Her shoulders were square. This was clearly a place where she felt safe. I was glad she still had that.

"Yeah," she said. "I mean . . . yeah."

"Look, it's none of my business, but if you want to know, you should ask your mother," I said.

"Know what?" Elizabeth asked.

"You know she came over to our house to fill out the divorce papers?" I said. Elizabeth winced and nodded. "They didn't ask me to leave the room. I didn't realize what they were talking about until they said it. They might have forgotten I was there. But you're not the reason your dad left. And I know you know that, but if you want the truth, you should ask."

"Is it Mum's fault?" Elizabeth's voice broke.

"Oh God, no," I said. I wanted to hug her, but I wasn't sure she'd let me. "No, sorry, that's not what I meant. Your mum is taking the high road. She's letting your dad keep secrets because she doesn't want you to think he's the bad guy. I don't think he'd do the same thing."

"She's covering for him?" Elizabeth asked. She looked too exhausted to be upset.

"Yeah," I said. "And she's telling herself it's for your sake, but it's not. Your dad asked her not to tell to protect you, but he's protecting himself. And neither you nor your mother deserves that."

"Do you think she'll tell me if I ask?" she said.

"I hope so," I told her. "Especially if you tell her what . . . happened at school."

"If I tell her what happened at school *and* she's been covering for Dad, she'll kill him," Elizabeth said. "Or she'll think it's her fault and that'll make her feel even worse."

"It is her fault," I said, a bit more harshly than I meant to. Elizabeth didn't flinch, though. "Not as much as your dad's, but she's the grown-up. They're both grown-ups. It's not your job."

"I don't know," Elizabeth said. She twisted her hands, and her shoulders started to round as she closed herself off from me. Then she took a deep breath. "But it's nice to have options. Thank you for coming over and letting me know."

"You're welcome," I said.

It hung there between us for a moment. She would have heard about what happened on the stairs. She could ask me, and I honestly have no idea if I'd be able to lie. Maddie's target was a thing, and Jenny's target was removed from her. Mine was personal. I put myself into it. It was much, much harder to keep it to myself. But I knew I had to.

"Thanks," she said again. "Is Elsie okay for beads? She mentioned something about weaving the last time she was here, but she talks a mile a minute. We've got some new ceramic stuff if you want to look."

"Sure," I said.

It wasn't fixed, entirely, because it could never be entirely fixed. But it was better than it had been.

Three weeks after my birthday, we did university applications. They called all the grade twelves to the cafeteria and sat us down, spaced out along the tables like we were at exams. The application form had three spaces for university and five for college. You didn't have to use all of them, but most kids filled out one or the other. The form had been free when my parents went to high school here, but now it was one hundred fifty dollars for university and one hundred ten for college. The school paid for most of it, thanks to a donation made several years ago from a member of the community who wished to remain anonymous (and was definitely my grandmother). Technically they weren't due until January, but ECSS always liked to get it over before Christmas in case there was sketchy weather after the holidays.

I flipped over the paper with the list of colleges. Ridgetown was close to the bottom. There was never any question of my going there. I wasn't going to run a farm. Also, Aaron would graduate before I got there, so there wouldn't be any point. I switched to the university page. There were plenty of accounting programs, but the one with the best co-op was at Carleton in Ottawa, more than six hours away. It wasn't the kind of university where you could come home for the weekend. Even a weekend like Thanksgiving would be pushing it.

I looked at my application form and neatly wrote Carleton down as my first choice, checking off the appropriate box for the program I wanted. Brock and Trent were my other two selections, but they weren't even safety schools. I had no doubts about my ability to get in where I wanted, but there was always a chance that someone would offer me a kick-ass scholarship, and I would take it, because Mum and Dad had six Sharpes to get educated.

I was one of the first people done, so I looked up and down the table at my classmates. Jen was writing with heavy strokes, too strong to be erased. I knew that she was very reluctantly writing down "Western" as one of her choices, even though she'd made it clear to her parents that humouring them by going on the campus tour did not mean she had changed her mind. Jenny was sitting with both the college and university forms in front of her. Grandma had paid for her application entirely, because Grandma was one of the few people Jenny would accept that sort of thing from (for herself, anyway. She'd let anyone do anything for her siblings). That meant she could do both the college and university applications, which was what Mrs. Kelly was encouraging her to do, because she wouldn't have to pay either fee. I knew that wouldn't help her decide, but I appreciated that she was being given the chance to make a decision.

Maddie set her pencil down, and Louise was half a second behind her. You hear all these horror stories about what American kids go through to apply to college. I literally thought it was something made up for TV to cause drama, but apparently some of them are true. Music, art, and drama programs require auditions, and some language courses require a placement test, but generally speaking, for us it's that easy: twenty minutes and then an early lunch. Jenny finally got writing. I couldn't see what, but she was definitely using both pieces of paper. We waited while she wrote, even as everyone else in the grade got up to take advantage of being early in line for food or just not being supervised for three minutes.

"Thanks guys," Jenny said, as we all walked out together. Mrs. Kelly was looking at her forms and smiling. None of us asked. She'd tell us when she was ready.

"How's your uncle liking his lunches here?" Jen asked, mostly to change the subject.

"He won't tell me about them," I said. "He said it's confidential, but that he thinks he might actually get through to one or two of them."

"Yeah, the ones whose parents think it's a real problem," Louise said.

"Sometimes you have to just take the win," I told her.

It wasn't easy. I'd spent my whole life trying to be the best, striving for perfection. Not in terms of grades or anything like that, but in some cosmic sense of the soul. And now I knew it wasn't possible. Maybe some saint who had lived on a mountaintop could do it, but Uncle David certainly couldn't, and neither could I. I would have to settle for the self-respect I'd built, and take everything else as it came. And God would have to take me, too, because I was done bending myself into the little Catholic shape I'd been brought up to believe He expected.

I'd been talking with Reverend Alden and, after I'd assured her that my uncle only found it mildly awkward, she had agreed to walk me through the Anglican version of confirmation to see if I liked it. I had no idea how it would turn out, but I was okay to go slowly. I'd always gone slowly with Aaron, too, and it was kind of nice, as we rushed towards the end of high school, to have a couple things in my life that were taking their time. I wasn't going to be a farmer, and I didn't know yet if I was going to be a farmer's wife, but I knew how to watch things grow.

FOURTH WISH:

Vandalism

(OR: LOUISE JANTZI'S 18TH BIRTHDAY)

16.

Louise Jantzi

Any hope we had of our last semester of high school being calm and uneventful was squashed the day before semester one ended. There were always two weird weeks in January before exams, but the second-semester sports teams started practicing as soon as the holiday break was over, because for some reason there were three sports seasons and two semesters. The schedule had not changed in generations. I was pretty sure my grandma had played basketball the same days I did.

ECSS was tiny. The pool our teams drew from was extremely limited, and while large high schools often had three teams for a given sport, at ECSS the junior team was often folded into the senior one for numbers. We usually managed to field three boys' basketball teams in the fall, but the girls' volleyball team was still in recovery from what had gone down with Isobel last year, so the juniors were added in. Traditionally, no grade nines were ever cut from the novice team so that everyone could get some experience.

And somehow, Mr. Carmichael thought with his whole chest that no one would notice when the novice team list was posted and only one name was missing.

He was too cowardly to warn them in advance, posting the list early in the morning so he wouldn't be in the hallway when someone saw it, because that would have involved talking to them

directly. Char had mentioned offhandedly one night as I was driving them home (Jenny was working) that practice felt weird because of the way Mr. Carmichael talked to other kids and around
them, but they hadn't seemed worried about it.

"I don't even mind if he says 'boys' or 'gentlemen,' " Char said.
"I know I'm on the boys' team. It feel like that's something I can
accept, you know?"

They had to say things like that to me and not Jenny, because
Jenny absolutely would not accept or pretend she knew. Still, Char
seemed confident as the tryout practices drew to a close.

Even though school hadn't started yet, it took approximately
zero seconds for word to spread through the halls that someone
had been cut and who it was, and then there was rampant specula-
tion as to why. Which was ridiculous, obviously, because everyone
knew why. They just weren't expecting someone to say the quiet
part out loud.

Mags's brother David, God love him, went straight to the
phys ed office to ask Mr. Carmichael for an explanation. Jenny
had driven to band that morning, which meant Char would be on
the bus, and that bus usually came in right before the bell rang at
8:55. David was in the office by 8:45, having gone straight to the
corkboard when he arrived.

Mags had been right behind him, but she and I waited outside because, to be perfectly honest, we were both really proud of
David and didn't want to step on his moment.

"Mr. Carmichael, I had a question about the basketball team,"
David said. "If you have a minute."

"I've got to do some photocopying before classes start," Mr.
Carmichael said. "I don't have much more than a minute."

He was so lucky Jenny was still in the music room. The phys ed office was only fifteen feet away from the door, so we could hear the band playing. As long as the music was still going, there probably wouldn't be a murder.

"You just made a mistake on the team list," David said. "It'll be super easy to fix."

"I didn't make a mistake," Mr. Carmichael said. "I know why you're here, and I think it's admirable, if entirely misplaced."

"Mr. Carmichael, no one gets cut from grade nine teams," David protested. "It's equal playing time. You said so at the first practice."

"I also have the ability to change my mind, Mr. Sharpe," Mr. Carmichael said. "Now, if you'll excuse me."

He pushed past David and walked right past me and Mags without so much as a glance. David wandered out of the office a few minutes later, looking shell-shocked.

"David, go and meet the bus," Mags said. "Char should hear it from you, not a whisper in the hallway."

David nodded, and took off down the hall. I realized it was quiet.

"Music room," I said.

"Oh my God," Mags said.

Mrs. Heskie was prickly about people interrupting practice, but there was so much organized chaos going on in the music room at the end of band practice that she barely even noticed we were there.

"What the hell?" Jenny said when we both grabbed her.

"Shut up and listen," I said. That got everyone's attention, and I realized that a bunch of people were listening in. Well, they'd all find out eventually anyway. And if I needed help restraining Jenny, I'd have it. "Carmichael posted the team list. Char's not on it."

"What?" Jenny said.

"It's not a mistake, either," Mags said. "David has already asked. He did it on purpose."

"No one gets cut from novice teams," Jenny protested. "It's equal playing time."

"No accounting for assholes," Emily Postma said. She was also watching Jenny closely. Emily was from town and had gone to school with the Hoernigs since kindergarten. Town kids tended to be way more protective of Char because they'd known them the longest. Emily's cop brother wasn't the only one in the family with a strong sense of justice; she was just better at it.

"Where are they?" Jenny demanded. Emily took the saxophone out of her hands and put it in the case.

"David's meeting the bus," I said.

"Neck strap!" said Emily when Jenny started to move. Jenny threw it at her and bolted.

"I'm on it," said Mags and followed her.

Jen and Maddie came over from the bass shelves, and I filled them in.

"Thanks, Emily," I said.

"No one needs to pay for a saxophone because they used it as a weapon," Emily said. "You better go help Mags."

By the time we got to the front door, Jenny was hugging a crying Char while David and Mags looked on kind of helplessly. We were right in the middle of the entryway, and kids were coming into the building and walking through the main hall, so we were definitely a traffic obstacle. I could tell from the looks Char was getting that the news was still spreading quickly.

"What are we going to do?" Jenny asked. "I mean, what do you want to do?"

"I should have just played for the girls," Char said.

"Carmichael coaches them, too," David pointed out. "He'd still probably be a dick."

"Should I talk to him?" Char asked.

"Not alone," Mags said quickly. "I mean, you want a witness and also moral support."

"We'll go," David said. "I'm not going to play if I don't like the answer."

"David," Char started, but he cut them off.

"I mean it!" David said. "I sat there and watched idiots run you out of church, and I will not do it again."

"Thanks, man," Char said. They reached for him, instinctively pulling back the moment they realized what they were doing. David took their hand in his own, and they smiled and wiped their face.

Mags and Jenny exchanged a look. We all knew David had a crush on Char when they were little, and we were all still young, but it certainly hadn't gotten *less* complicated.

The first bell rang. We had five minutes to make it to class, and I knew Jen hadn't eaten breakfast yet because she usually got a cookie from the cafeteria. I got a granola bar out of my bag and handed it to her.

"Thanks, Louise," she said. It was even chocolate chip.

"Jenny, you good?" I asked tentatively, trying to close my backpack with my arm still through one of the straps. Maddie stepped over and did it for me.

"No," Jenny said. "But Char can handle this on their own. For now."

I hoped that wherever in the building Mr. Carmichael was hiding, he felt a chill run down his spine.

"Let's go," Jenny said. "I'm not adding a late slip to this mess."

None of us had ever gotten a late slip. Not because we were never late, but because none of the teachers ever bothered. We were good girls. We were in clubs and on teams. If we were late, we probably had a reason. And it happened so rarely.

"The volleyball lists were posted, too," Mags said. "I forgot to read them, though."

"I don't care," said Jenny, who cared a lot.

"We'll check later," Maddie said as we started up the blessedly quiet central staircase.

We peeled off to go to our classes, Mags hovering over Jenny as they headed up for calculus. I didn't know how any of us were going to focus that morning, but it turned out to not matter.

It was the last day of the semester, so even though it was a Friday in the middle of January, there was a casual feel to the day. We had worksheets and the traditional trivia contests in Mr. Attis's classes, but generally time seemed to go quickly. I wasn't particularly sorry to leave any of my first semester classes behind. Next semester I had a co-op split between the day care and the library, and they were going to pay me. We all just had to get through exams next week, and then we'd be one step closer to graduating and moving on.

We'd also be one step closer to my birthday, which was on January 27. The girls tried to plan something big every year because I usually planned theirs. Now that Mags was a better baker, it was slightly less disastrous, but the truth was I didn't mind if I had to plan my own birthday. My house was the best for parties, and I loved making cakes. I didn't even have to do the dishes, because Mum and Dad wanted Paul to learn responsibility, so they made him do it. It was going to come together very nicely. The only thing I'd been worried about was that I didn't know what I was going to do for my wish.

And now, no thanks to Mr. Carmichael, I definitely, definitely did.

17.
Louise Jantzi

It was even worse than we'd thought. It turned out that while Mr. Carmichael had been "uncomfortable" about having Char on the team, he hadn't been planning to do anything about it until several students and their parents complained. With their backup, he'd found the courage to be the bigot he was at heart because he'd be able to lay all the responsibility at their feet. David and all the other kids from town had quit the team immediately, along with a couple other boys who had gotten to know Char since September and were willing to make a stand. Mr. Carmichael had numbers on his side. He still had nine kids left for the team, so he could lose seven happily, and those who remained would get more playing time, so they were happy, too.

Mr. Kelly, the junior coach, invited David and his friends to practice with his team. There were ten juniors, and all of them were better than the grade nines were, but this would give them a chance to work with a real coach, and they could try out again next year. Char was not invited, so the boys turned down the offer.

Julia Hoernig closed the store in order to come in for a meeting with Mrs. Fiske. Jenny said her mum hadn't wanted to talk about it, but had obviously been frustrated with whatever Mrs. Fiske said.

"Probably some bullshit about having to hear both sides,"

Maddie said. "Or following the rules so they can compete in the conference playoffs."

"They're not going to make it to the conference playoffs," Jenny said. "Half of them can't even dribble the damn ball."

Char requested that no one make a fuss, but Jenny definitely knew which kids and which parents were involved—they weren't even hiding it—and I knew she'd plan something if no one else stepped in. Fortunately, we had my birthday party the weekend before my actual birthday, which meant I could intervene before the new semester started.

Sunny Saturdays in January feel rare, but I wasn't going to complain when I got one. I got up early because I wanted to try a new cake recipe, and there was a good chance I'd mess it up a couple of times before I made something I was willing to share. I had a reputation to protect, after all, and I'd convinced Mags she was off the hook for planning my party since our exam schedule gave me a bit of free time at the end of the week. Mum had got all the ingredients I'd requested, so I put on my headphones and started baking. By the time my family came down to the kitchen for breakfast, I had made scones, too, which Paul always appreciated.

"I love not being dairy farmers," he said, helping himself to two scones and getting the raspberry jam out of the fridge.

"You don't even remember being a dairy farmer," Dad told him. "But you're right."

Dad made eggs, and then he and Paul went to the barn.

"I'll get the frying pan when I get the rest of your stuff," Paul said, making a face on the way out the door.

"If you'd learn how to cook, you'd wash fewer dishes," I reminded him.

"Absolutely not," Paul said. "I will wash every dish in the world to avoid cooking."

"You know, that's an acceptable deal," Mum said.

"Why are you even awake?" I asked. She got home at six this morning because she was on a night rotation.

"Scones, obviously," she said with her mouth full. "What time will the girls be here?"

"Two-ish, I think?" I said. "Jenny has to work until three, and I don't know how Mags is getting here. We might sleep out there, if that's okay?"

"Yeah, I think we can trust you," Mum said. "Just explain it to the pizza guy if it's after nine because your brother will be wearing headphones and your dad will be asleep in front of the TV. And leave some of the chips for Sunday. Paul has people coming over in the evening for some game."

"Will do," I said. "Please go to bed."

"Now that your dad's gone, I'm going to starfish the whole thing," she said, shuffling towards the stairs.

I went back to the cake. The first one was probably fine, but I didn't like the colour of the caramel and I felt like the pastry could have been flakier. Knowing that Paul was having company, I put the whole thing in the freezer instead of keeping it for the pigs. His friends were all gross fifteen-year-old boys who would eat literally anything, but they loved me for baking, even when they only got the mistakes.

Two hours or so later, I was leaning up against the kitchen is-land eating cold scrambled eggs and waiting for the timer to ding. Everything was coated in a light dusting of icing sugar, which made the air taste sweet. I kept calling it a cake, but it was actually mille-feuille stacked up a bit higher than usual, like a crêpe cake. I had no idea how we were going to cut it, but it smelled fantastic. With the pastry settling, I started working on the cream and a second batch of caramel. This time, I was satisfied with how it turned out, so I built all the layers up carefully instead of just slapping everything together like I had for the boys.

I cheerfully left a giant mess for Paul, put the cake in the cold room, and went upstairs to shower and wash the icing sugar out of my hair. Maddie showed up at one because her dad was working and her mother had decided to go shopping in London, so she couldn't have a car.

"She can help you set up!" Mrs. Carter called out as Maddie got out of the car.

"Have fun, Mother," Maddie said, firmly closing the car door. "Don't worry, Louise. I wouldn't dream of interfering in whatever you've got planned."

I laughed, and we both headed over to the barn. There had been a 4-H meeting on Friday night, so we had to rearrange all the couches and beanbag chairs. It was definitely handy having a second person for that. We went through the chip selection and picked out all the best ones while still technically leaving plenty for Paul. By the time Maddie was emptying the first set of ice cubes into the bucket and refilling the trays, Jen and Mags showed up.

"Jenny texted," Mags said.

"I haven't checked my phone," I told her. "Is everything okay?"

"Yeah, she's just getting out of work at two, so she'll be here by two twenty," Jen said.

"What time is it?" I asked.

"Two fifteen," Maddie said.

"Oh, for Pete's sake," I said. "I wanted to, like, have a plan before she got here, but I don't think five minutes is enough time."

"A plan for what?" Jen asked.

"Not so much a plan, I guess," I corrected myself. "More like . . . permission? I didn't want to get Jenny's hopes up."

"Permission for what?" Jen poured herself a glass of orange pop and set the cream soda out for Mags.

"I know the whole thing with the wishes is that they're supposed to be anonymous," I said. "Like, we don't want anything to get traced back to us, and that makes sense."

"Yeah," said Maddie. I saw the moment comprehension dawned. "Oh yeah, I don't know."

"Char?" Jen clarified.

"Yeah," I said.

"We'd have to be extra careful," Mags said. "The last two have been a little bit of freestyle, and we were able to leave things to chance. This is going to have to be more like the sod poisoning. We're going to have to be organized."

We heard Jenny's car pull into the driveway and come to a stop near the barn. A few seconds later, she appeared over the top of the ladder. Without meaning to, we all looked at her expectantly.

"Hi," Jenny said. "You're acting like it's my birthday, not Louise's."

"Everybody get a drink and sit down," I said.

Maddie switched the cream soda for the root beer that she and Jenny preferred, and I went straight for the Coke. There were bowls of chips all over the place, and it took another moment for us to make sure everyone had the kind they liked. Then Jenny looked at me.

"Okay, I'm starting to get nervous," she said. "What's up?"

"It's my birthday wish," I told her. "I've been thinking about it ever since Mags's birthday, and I didn't know what to do. But then two weeks ago, the thing with Char and the basketball team happened, and we were all so mad about it. And I know that Char doesn't want anyone to make a fuss, but what if, like, unknown citizens made a fuss?"

"Louise, I will light fires if I am allowed," Jenny said.

"I was thinking about that, too," I told her. I turned to face everyone else. "The targets are Mr. Carmichael and all the boys who stayed on the team. If I could get their parents, I would, but I think that might be asking too much, so we'll have to settle for the people at school."

"We'll have to be careful," Jenny said.

"We already decided that," Jen said.

"You decided before I got here?" Jenny asked.

"I took an opinion poll in the approximate five minutes I had before you got here," I explained. "I didn't want to get your hopes up if we decided it was too risky."

"I appreciate that," she said. "So we're careful. And we try to leave as few things to chance as possible. That probably means I can't light anyone on fire."

"Well, no," I said. I took a deep breath. "It has to be something striking and targeted. Something like how we poisoned the sod, but on a quicker timeline. How do you feel about acid?"

18.

Louise Jantzi

It was audacious and possibly insane, and we might actually get caught. None of us minded. We had been successful three times, and it made us confident. Still scared, which kept us humble enough to be careful, but confident enough to aim high.

I had not expected to spend my eighteenth birthday party researching what kinds of cleaning chemicals could be used to ruin cloth, but here we were, flipping through the MSDS sheets for all the chemicals my dad used in the barn. It turned out that a lot of soaps and cleaners could, if used in high enough concentrations, destroy cloth. Which made sense. They used to use lye in soap, but you could also use it to dissolve a corpse, if you had the time. We focused on things we thought would be available in the janitorial room, which was down the hall from the phys ed office.

The actual idea had come from Jenny, though as soon as she started talking, I knew exactly what she meant. ECSS didn't have much of a budget for sports, so we used the same uniforms every year. The uniforms worn by the novice basketball teams were barely holding together anymore, because they were so old.

"We just have to find out which parent is doing the laundry, and what day," Jenny said. "And then sneak into the phys ed office, put the box on Carmichael's desk, and pour the acid over top of it."

"It's too bad we couldn't do it when he was marking exams," Jen mused. "God, can you imagine if he lost the entire grade twelve health class?"

"I'll take what we can get," I said. "And I'll make sure that the Students' Council budget can't pay for new uniforms. They'll have to use something gross and super dated that's been in storage in the gun range since the late 80s."

"I think I've got something," Maddie said, looking up from the booklet she was reading. "Acetone. It's a common cleaner, and it has to be diluted by the user. You remember that part of chemistry, right, Mags? All the labels and stuff?"

"Yes," Mags said. "Though there's probably a 4-H unit on that somewhere in here if we need a refresher."

There was, and by the time we'd all managed to read it, we were starving, so I ordered the pizzas. It was the owner, not one of the kids, so he knew where to direct the taxi, and our food showed up before we ran out of chips.

"So, theoretically," Jenny said, stretching cheese and grinning, "if we were ordering pizza for someone who can't eat pepperoni or ham, do we have to find a special restaurant?"

"She also can't have cheese and beef," Jen said primly, loading up on Hawaiian. "Together, I mean. And honestly, I don't know. We usually eat at her house, for simplicity. She eats the vegetarian pizza when it's at school, though."

"Jennifer Dalrymple, I am SHOCKED," Maddie said, throwing a pillow at her. "How long has this been going on, exactly?"

"About a month," Jen admitted. "She's a bit nervous, I think. We've talked about it. It's like, if she were a boy, it would be easier to conceptualize, but instead she's a girl."

Mags was nodding.

"Aaron's easy, because he was on the edges anyway," I said. "But Dahlia is also our friend, she's just not part of this."

I indicated the entire room with a pointed slice of Canadian.

"Yeah," Jen said. "So we're working it out."

"That's so mature of you," Jenny said. "I'm very proud."

"Shut up," said Jen.

"And you can't tell her," Maddie said. "Even after what happened in the stairwell."

"Yeah, that part's hard, too." Jen stopped smiling. "You know I wouldn't, right? I would never."

"We know," Jenny assured her. "I am going to continue to tease the hell out of you, though. This is the best thing that's ever happened to me."

"Or it will be until David works up his courage about Char." Mags grinned. "Right now he's trying to figure out if he's still straight."

"You know, I don't actually know how that works," Jenny said.

"Do not ask Char," Mags said. "David will die. And I want to witness this."

"I think it's time for cake," I said. "And it took forever, so I hope you all like it."

"Louise, have we ever not liked something you baked?" Maddie asked.

"Fair point," I said, and went to get the knife.

The thing I forgot to account for was that the uniforms ECSS purchased for their athletes were made almost entirely of polyester, which was popular because it was essentially unkillable. A 70 percent solution of sulphuric acid wouldn't do it, and even a fire has to be 250 degrees centigrade. We would need to see a tag in order to figure out if there was any cotton at all involved, and then we'd know if we'd be able to use something readily available, like acetone. It would be nice and dramatic to completely destroy all the uniforms, but we'd settle for making a giant mess on Mr. Carmichael's desk and rendering them unwearable.

"I wish David hadn't turned his uniform in so quickly," Mags said while we brainstormed how to get our hands on one of the shirts.

"Curse that boy's sense of morality," I said. Jenny snickered, and Mags rolled her eyes.

"Oh, shit," Jen said. She sat up straight, and I knew she had found both a solution and another problem.

"Dahlia Hastings's brother is on the junior boys' basketball team," Maddie said. She'd clearly figured that out a while ago, but hadn't brought it up.

We all waited for Jenny to say something, but instead she looked at Jen sympathetically.

"Jen, I don't think you should," Jenny said. "We'll find an alternative. I don't want you to risk something of yours, even for Char."

"She might not have to," Mags said. "Every time Zac Hastings visits his grandfather after school, he puts his backpack on the bed and takes him for a walk. Zac can hold him up, but there's not enough space in the room for the upright walker, so they go to one of the activity areas. They're usually gone for about twenty minutes."

"Do you have that whole place cased out?" I asked. I wouldn't put it past her.

"Not on purpose," Mags said. "It runs on routine, you know, and I'm there at the same time practically every time I visit, so the same things are always happening."

"You don't mind going through his bag?" Jen asked.

"Nope," Mags said. "If anyone catches me, I'll just say Grandpa jostled the bed and knocked it on the floor."

"Does he do that now?" Maddie asked, suddenly concerned. "I thought he was pretty steady on his feet."

"The doctor said it's normal," Mags said. "He's atrophying, because if no one makes him move around, he doesn't. Even with Grandma there all the time, he's nowhere near as active as he was when he was on the farm. It was always going to be a downhill slide."

"It still sucks," I said.

"I need more cake," said Jen. There was a murmur of general agreement. "I can't believe you made something this fancy, Louise. This is bakery stuff."

"It did take me more than one try," I reminded her. "And I've made this kind of pastry before. Just not so much of it."

"It's incredible," Mags said. "Don't let me eat any more or I will die."

"There's a fruit tray in the fridge," I told her. "And there's still pizza if you need protein."

Mags went foraging, and Jen dug into an incredibly large piece of cake. I didn't mean to food-shame, but at a certain point, I had to worry about her pancreas.

Mags and Jenny hashed out Mags's plan for the nursing home. It would require some specific timing, since Zac wouldn't have his uniform with him on any random day. Mags would have to be there alone, too, instead of with one of her siblings.

"The day before a game," I said. "The girls usually wash their own uniforms, because we're not incompetent, but when we did it as a group, they were always handed back out the day before a game."

"We just have to hope he doesn't leave it in his locker," Maddie said.

"He won't if there's a spirit day," Jenny said.

"I hate those things." I groaned. "They're so stupid. The uniforms are uncomfortable enough without wearing them all morning."

"But Zac would definitely take the shirt home," Jen said. "And hopefully stop at the nursing home on the way."

"I'll put it together," I said. "It's the beginning of the season, so it won't look weird. Students' Council will go for it because what else are we going to do?"

"Sell Valentine's candy?" Jenny suggested.

"Ugh, don't remind me," I said.

Mags finished her pizza and went to the bathroom. When she came back, she was in her pajamas, and she started to make a nest in one of the beanbag chairs.

"You don't need to go to bed," she said. "I'm just stuffed, and I don't want to move again."

"It's a good idea," Maddie said. "We can put on a movie and yell at it until we fall asleep."

The Jantzi collection of DVDs and even a few working VHS tapes was legendary, and I was more than happy to dig through the pile while everyone else got changed. Eventually I came up with the first Tom Cruise *Mission: Impossible* movie, which we had on a disc even though it was definitely old enough to be on tape.

"Ah, a classic of the genre," Jen said as the FBI warning flashed up. "How does that even work if we're Canadian?"

"I have no idea," Mags said. "They used to show these things at the library on Sundays in the summer, and it was definitely not legal, but no one ever really did anything."

"Pause it until I get back," I said, grabbing my toiletry bag. "I like the beginning the best."

I heard the playback stop and the chatter resume before I closed the bathroom door. It was cozy out here away from the house, with no one to care how late we stayed up or what we did. And they always assumed that we were behaving. I knew we'd earned that, but it felt increasingly ridiculous as time went on. Amelia Chaser had earned things. Char Hoernig should have.

I brushed my teeth, even though I still had some Coke left, and braided my hair up to keep it out of my face—and Maddie's, since she had put her sleeping bag down beside me. When I came back out, the lamps were off, but there was plenty of light from the TV. Jenny waited until I was settled in before she hit play again. It was a reassuring movie. The good guys were going to win, even though they'd been wronged. And it didn't matter that they were going to break the law to do it.

Probably not the lesson I was supposed to learn. But I learned it.

19.
Louise Jantzi

Mags and I ended up going to the nursing home together. It wasn't an official decision or anything, more like we'd just decided that no one was going to do anything alone. Especially not something that involved family members. The nursing home was way too hot, but most of the people who lived there didn't move around much, so they were still wrapped in blankets and sweaters.

"Hello, Louise," Mags's grandma said. "I didn't know you were coming today."

"I miss him, too," I said. It was as good an explanation as any, and it was the truth.

"He's doing pretty well today," Mrs. Shropshall said. She pulled on her mittens and a touque. Mags handed her her heavy coat off the back of the chair. "He's just quiet."

"All right," Mags said. "We were going to sit here, if that's okay?"

"Don't mess up my knitting." She gestured to the bed, where her overflowing craft basket was leaning up against the footboard.

"We'll stay clear," I promised.

"Where's Mr. Hastings?" Mags asked, like it was completely natural.

"Oh, he's out for a walk with Zac," Mrs. Shropshall said. "They left about five minutes ago. I think Zac said something about the back activity room, but they made cookies this afternoon, so I'd be willing to bet they're in the front instead."

With that, she was off. It must be so weird, splitting your life between two places. I guess that kids with separated parents did it all the time, but you don't usually expect adults to have to. She couldn't live here because she didn't need to, and if she stayed home, part of her life would always be missing. On top of everything else, she had to go home to a quiet house. I knew she was at the main house a lot, and preferred the solitude sometimes, but still. It had to hurt.

"Hi, Grandpa," Mags said.

David looked up at her, his eyes glassy.

"Is it time for dinner?" he asked. "I think my wife was here, but she had to go somewhere."

"No," Mags said. "I'm just here to visit with my friend."

"Hi, Mr. Shropshall," I said.

"You're about my granddaughter's age, aren't you?" he said.

"Yes," I told him. "We go to school together."

"There were five of you," he said. Then he laughed. "That's why I always said you were a handful."

Mags swallowed hard, and even I had to blink a few times.

"That's right," I said. "You played with us a lot."

"I should look through the backpack," Mags said. I think she wanted something to do with her hands. "Keep an eye on the door, would you?"

"Sure," I said.

Mags's grandpa kept talking to me, mostly about the yard at the farm. Mrs. Shropshall wasn't kidding about it being a good day. He seemed to remember the trees and gardens exactly, even though he was about ten years behind, because he kept coming back to a maple tree that had been taken down when we were in grade two.

Mags picked Zac's backpack up off the chair and gingerly pulled the zipper open. Fortunately, Zac was tidy, and kept his backpack fairly organized. The uniform wasn't in the biggest pocket, but Mags could see that right away, so she didn't waste time before opening the second zipper. She pulled out the shirt and checked the tag.

"Thirty percent cotton, seventy percent polyester," she said. Quickly, she refolded the shirt and put it back in the bag. She closed the zippers and carefully placed the backpack where it had been on the chair. "Is that going to work?"

"From what I can tell, yes," I said. "The cotton is much more vulnerable than the polyester, but with that mix, something that affects one will affect the other."

"Now we just have to make sure none of us gets an incriminating chemical burn," she said, coming back over to sit beside me on the bed.

"Do you know my granddaughter, too?" Mr. Shropshall asked Mags.

The research on dementia was always changing, which made sense because more and more people were living longer. Some people recommended humouring the patient; some recommended correction. My mother said that it was some combination of whatever was least upsetting for everyone involved, and she was probably correct.

"Yes," Mags said.

"Good," her grandpa said. "Good, she always had such good friends."

"When do you think is the best time tomorrow?" I asked,

partially to keep Mags on an even keel and partially because this was as good a place as any to talk. "There's band practice, so the others will be at school early."

"No," Mags said. "Mrs. Heskie will notice if they're not there. And the boys won't turn their uniforms in again until after the game."

"Right," I said, reworking the schedule in my mind: today we check the tag, tomorrow is spirit day and the game, tomorrow night is laundry.

"Mrs. Aberfoyle does the washing," Mags said.

"Of course she does," I said. Her son Curtis had been bragging that he was the one who started the whole process of getting Char removed by telling his parents about how uncomfortable he felt playing ball with them. I didn't care if it was true. The kid was still an asshole, and his parents were just mean.

"Curtis is on one of the earlier busses, at least," Mags said. "But we might have to do this at lunch."

"There's another option," I said, considering it. "I could do it right after the start of third period and be late for co-op."

I watched Mags consider it for a moment. I wouldn't have an alibi, and someone from co-op would notice I was late. Unless I claimed to have driven to the wrong building or something, but that was unlike me.

"Let's save that for a last resort," Mags said.

"You girls have strange problems," Mr. Shropshall said, suddenly focused back on us. "Are you okay?"

He sounded so much like he had before, sharp and right on topic, that for a moment, I thought we'd be caught out. Mags looked at him with a mixture of alarm and hope that was painful to witness. Then he blinked again, and it was gone.

"Have you seen my wife?" he asked. "She usually takes me to dinner, and I think it's almost time for dinner."

"She just went for a quick walk outside," Mags said. "You know she likes to get fresh air before she eats."

"That she does." He leaned back in his chair and closed his eyes. Mags let out a long breath.

Before she could say anything else, Zac and his grandfather came around the corner. She jumped up to make sure the path was clear for them.

"Thank you, Mags," Mr. Hastings said on his way past. It was hard for him to talk when he was walking, but he always tried to be polite.

Zac helped him get settled in his chair and then put the walker out in the hallway. When he came back in, he picked up his backpack without noticing anything was different.

"So," he said, turning to look at us with a grin. "Are we, like, related now?"

Mags burst into giggles. Zac knew it wasn't that funny, so he looked a little confused. I could understand perfectly, though. Stress bubbling over does weird things. Even I felt like laughing, and I didn't usually tease the others. Too much.

"Is this how I find out my granddaughter has a girlfriend?" Mr. Hastings asked, also starting to laugh.

"Oh my God, I thought you knew about Jen," Zac said. "Dahlia said she tells you everything!"

"She didn't tell me this!" Mr. Hastings said. His smile lit up his whole face.

Just as our laughter was starting to die down, a different sound filled the room. Sitting in his chair, watching the world go by without seeming to notice much of it, David Shropshall started to sing

"My Funny Valentine." Mags's grandma came back into the room just as he finished the first part, and squeezed Mags's shoulders while they listened to the rest. She had taken off her mitts and hat when she came back inside, but her nose and cheeks were still rosy. As he got to the last two lines, Mr. Shropshall looked right at her.

"That was very nice, David," Mrs. Shropshall said when he was done. "I love it when you sing."

"He sings to me sometimes," Mr. Hastings said. "Or maybe it's to himself and I'm just here, but I like to imagine it's on purpose. It's a lot of hymns, so I don't know them, but it's very soothing."

"That's so cool," Zac said. "I mean, I wish everything was better, but it's cool that he still likes singing."

The nurse came in with everyone's predinner meds, and Mags, Zac, and I took that as our cue to clear out. We stopped in the vestibule to get our outside clothes back on, and watched as the first few residents were wheeled or walked in for dinner. Sometimes it was sad and sometimes it was just nothing, and I wasn't sure which was worse.

"Do you need a ride?" I asked Zac. "Since we're cousins or whatever now?"

Mags gave me a small smile, which was all I wanted.

"No," he said. "I'm going to walk home. It's not that far."

Mags and I got in the car and we set out towards her house, the opposite direction from mine.

"I'm going to get my G2," she said. "I'll schedule the test when I get home."

"You don't have to," I said. "Not driving is fine."

"I know," she said. "I just want to be as mobile as possible for as long as possible."

"Fair enough," I said.

We didn't talk the rest of the way to her house. I could only guess what Mags was thinking about—responsibility and mobility and freedom—but I was only thinking about the distance between the janitorial room and the phys ed office. Sometimes the smallest movements were the hardest.

20.
Louise Jantzi

The phys ed office was supposed to be locked, but there were so many teachers who taught other subjects in addition to PE that they didn't always bother because at any given time, half of them were sending a student to pick up something they'd forgotten anyway. In this case, it was Mr. Kelly, who also taught algebra, and happened to have forgotten his chalk holder. This wasn't his fault. The other room he taught math in had a whiteboard. When he asked for a volunteer, Jenny all but threw herself in the air. When we assembled at Mags's locker for lunch, she had the intel we needed.

"The box is on Carmichael's desk," she said as we huddled around her.

"I have even better news," Maddie announced. "They couldn't get a sub to cover Mr. Rogman this afternoon when the volleyball teams go to Exeter. I heard them talking in the office when I dropped off attendance for English. They're going to give us a free period, we just have to tell them where we're spending it."

"The music room," Jen said. "There's no class there during third, so we'll be able to use a practice room. Mrs. Heskie will be upstairs teaching French. As long as all the doors are unlocked, we've got it."

Like the other times, it was all coming together. And it would have to, because this time, not only was it personal, no one would dismiss it as a coincidence. The memorial at the church was a mystery. What happened to Trevor was weird. The boys in the hallway getting caught by two priests was just pure luck. But this was going to be very obviously deliberate. We couldn't make it look like an accident. They would be looking for a culprit. We had to make sure they didn't find us.

"I don't like that all four of you will be here and I'll be gone," I said. I had to leave for co-op in about fifteen minutes. "You can't even text me. I'll have to wait until the end of the day."

"Unless you hear police sirens," Jenny said.

"Don't even." I closed my eyes and took a breath. Maddie had done most of Jenny's wish. Mags and Jenny had done all of Maddie's. I could handle this.

"We'll be fine," Maddie said. I looked at her and saw that she wasn't just trying to patronize me. "We'll be careful, and we'll be fine."

"All right," I said. "Please understand that this is about to be the worst afternoon of my whole life."

"Are you at the library today?" Jen asked. I nodded. "Then I'll stop in on my way home. You can just wait for me there."

"Okay," I said. The alarm on my phone beeped. "Good luck."

It was time to go.

I regretted every single one of my life's decisions before I even got to the car. If I weren't going into early childhood education, I wouldn't need a co-op. If I didn't have a co-op, I wouldn't be leaving school right now. If I weren't leaving school right now, I could help.

The task didn't need all five of us. It didn't even need four. At most we needed someone to carry the bottle and someone to keep an eye out. The back stairwell echoed so loudly that anyone coming down it would be heard a mile away, so only the halls needed to be watched. You could stand in the corner, hidden by the cloakroom at the front of the music room, and see both directions without anyone seeing you. There wasn't anywhere to hide in the hallway, but it was a short distance between the janitorial room and the phys ed office.

I focused on driving so I didn't accidentally crash into a telephone pole or something. The library ran a children's program on Tuesday and Thursday afternoons, which is why I split my time between there and the day care. The kids just came down half a block and got to play with different toys, do different crafts, and read different books. It was incredibly popular.

It took ten minutes to leave school, drive, and park. By the time I got out of the car, the bell at the end of lunch would be ringing. Five minutes after that, Mr. Rogman's chemistry students would be set free. Then the four of them would have seventy-six minutes to get the job done.

I honestly do not recall how I got through the afternoon without stepping on someone or giving almond milk to the wrong kid. I was on autopilot, and I thought for sure it would be noticed, but no one suspected that anything was up. I thought maybe I'd calm down when I knew that third period was over and fourth was beginning, but somehow that only made it worse. At least there weren't any sirens.

By 3:15, I was outside on the bench. It was freezing cold, but I felt like if I stayed in the library a moment longer, I'd explode. I had mittens and a headband, but I was still blowing on my hands to keep them warm. I didn't want to sit in the car. When Jen's car pulled around the corner, I jumped to my feet and met her at the edge of the sidewalk.

"We're all fine," she started off. I could see Maddie in the passenger seat, and she certainly looked fine. "It's done and we're fine. Do you want to follow me home?"

Jen's house would be empty until at least five, when her parents would be home from the elementary school.

"Oh my God, yes," I said. "I'll be right behind you."

Jen drove off and I jumped in my car. Now that I knew they'd been successful, I could calm down a little bit. My brain was still going a mile a minute, but at least I was no longer running disaster scenarios.

"We're in the kitchen!" Jen shouted when I crashed through the front door of her house.

I ditched my boots and coat and headed back.

"Tell me everything," I said, climbing up onto a stool next to the kitchen island.

"Here." Jen passed me a hot chocolate and opened a bag of cheese bread sticks. "Okay, so the short version is—"

"She doesn't want the short version," Maddie said. "She wants me to tell her that you almost died and then draw the whole thing out."

"You almost WHAT?" I demanded, choking on a mouthful of cheese bread.

"See?" Maddie said. Jen started laughing.

"Someone had better start talking," I said. "I have had a very stressful afternoon."

"Okay, so we got to the music room as planned," Jen said. "Mags went out to check the doors while the rest of us put our instruments together. When she came back, she said we were all good to go."

I forced myself to calm down, mostly because I liked cheese

bread and didn't want to aspirate it, but also because I didn't want to miss anything they told me.

"Then Jen and I went to the janitorial room." Maddie took over. "I went in, because I knew what the label was going to look like."

"And then just as she got the bottle off the shelf, Mr. Kreskin came in," Jen said.

"Oh my God," I said. Mr. Kreskin was definitely the nicest janitor at ECSS, but even he would have questions about kids stealing acetone.

"Jen was amazing," Maddie said. "She spun this whole story about how she'd spilled a juice box on the risers and we had paper towels, but she was worried it was going to be sticky, and we came for a mop and bucket, but no one was here because janitors need lunch, too."

"And that gave Maddie enough time to actually get the mop and bucket," Jen said. "I told him we'd use the sink in the music room, and off we went."

"Where was the bottle?" I asked.

"Under the mop," Maddie told me. "It ended up being perfect because we didn't really have a plan for what to do with the bottle afterwards, but now we had an excuse to go back to the janitor's room."

I wanted to put my head between my knees and breathe deeply, but the stool was too high. I slumped over the counter instead. I had way too much adrenaline considering I hadn't been there. Not being there was the worst.

"Anyway, so then Maddie went in and dumped about half the bottle on top of the uniforms and I took the bucket to the music room," Jen said. "I filled it with enough water that it'd look like it had been wet, doused the mop, waited about five minutes, and then took the whole thing back and put the bottle on the shelf where Maddie told me to."

"I dusted my hands with baking soda that Jenny brought and then washed my hands for like an hour," Maddie said. "But to be perfectly honest, the disinfectant we use on the mouthpieces could have been my excuse if anyone thought I smelled like a chemical."

"Mr. Carmichael didn't get back to his office until way after the end of third period, because he had his class out snowshoeing," Jen said. "We were all up on the second floor, so I don't know what sort of commotion there was, but I heard from Dahlia who heard from Zac who heard from Mr. Kelly telling Mrs. Fiske about it that Carmichael's desk will have to be decontaminated."

"And Char was in class the entire time," Maddie finished triumphantly.

I know I'm the Mom Friend. People who don't know us assume it's Mags, but they're wrong. I'm the one who knows everyone's schedules and what to bring them if they miss breakfast. I'm the one who remembers every allergy and preference. I'm the one who reminds them to fill up their water bottles. They did all of this without me, and they were fine. I'm both hurt and a little proud.

"Are you okay?" Jen asked. "I know you like to be around when we do stuff."

It's as close as she'll get to admitting that I'm the one who takes care of them.

"Yeah," I said. I took a long drink of hot chocolate, warming up literally and metaphorically. "Let's never do it again."

Maddie looked at Jen.

"Let's only do it one more time," I corrected.

Four for four.

FIFTH WISH:

Blackmail

(OR: JEN DALRYMPLE'S 18TH BIRTHDAY)

21.
Jen Dalrymple

I don't usually spend much time thinking about my birthday, but this particular year, I was glad that it wasn't until May. The weeks after Louise's birthday were super intense. I played it off because Maddie didn't seem too affected, but I was seriously stressed by almost getting caught in the janitorial room. And, to be quite honest, kind of alarmed at how easy it was for me to lie to someone I genuinely respected.

When Maddie had originally talked about how no one would ever suspect us, I had kind of shrugged it off. It wasn't until I was standing in the doorway, looking Mr. Kreskin in the face while Maddie stood behind me with a bottle of high-concentrate acetone in her hands, that I truly understood what she'd meant. Mags had mentioned something about it, too, how it never even occurred to her uncle that she'd step out of line, but for me it was more than that. We should have gotten caught. Mr. Kreskin should have put the pieces together, even though we'd been careful not to use so much acid that it would be super noticeable if someone checked the bottle. But he bought my story completely. Mrs. Fiske didn't even interview us as potential witnesses because we were down the hallway when the "incident" took place. It was eye-opening, and I wasn't entirely sure how I felt about it.

At the very least, I was not in a hurry for it to be my turn. I had plenty of other things to keep myself busy, and frankly we could do with a couple of quiet months. I was thinking about it, obviously, considering targets like they were clay pigeons at the Fish & Game, but I wasn't close to making a decision, and I didn't want to be. We had to pick universities soon. And there were other things that I was working on.

My first objective was summer vacation. Or, rather, how I wanted my summer to not *be* a vacation. My parents both guard their off-school time, and usually during March Break or whatever, we're gone. Eganston Elementary gets them for more than twelve hours a day, five days a week, ten months of the year, but the rest of their time is theirs. They'd started backpacking after teacher's college, way before they met each other—the sort of travel where the expensive thing was the airline ticket, and then trains and hostels were cheap. They'd upgraded a little bit since then, but the wanderlust was still the same. I liked that, because I do like to travel, but this year I wanted to make money.

"I've been thinking," I said, hopefully casually and not like I'd been rehearsing in the shower for the past few weeks in preparation for this very conversation at the dinner table. "It's going to be your tenth anniversary this summer. Maybe you should go someplace really cool, like Italy."

"That is on my bucket list," Mum said. Dad smiled at her. God, I loved having a dad that smiled at my mum. "Is that where you want to go?"

"That's actually what I wanted to talk to you about," I said. I set down my fork and took a breath. "I think you should go without me. Not just because it's a special anniversary, but because I want to have a job. I don't want to go to university without spending money or, like, being able to maintain a schedule."

My parents exchanged a look across the table. Even though they've only had a decade to practice, they're very good at the talking-without-talking thing. Maybe it comes from all the effort they expend not swearing in front of their students.

"What sort of job were you thinking?" Dad asked.

"I want to apply to be one of the student leaders with the Sparling Young Company," I said. "They run theatre camps for little kids all summer, so even if you haven't acted with them before, you can still apply."

"You'd need one of the cars for that," Mum said. "Which I guess wouldn't be a problem if we were in Italy."

I tried not to look too guilty. That had definitely been part of my calculation.

"I'll pay for gas," I said. "I might need an assist with grocery money, though."

"Sweetheart, you know that I always want to be a family of three, right?" Dad asked. He looked at me like he had ten years ago, when he asked me if he could marry my mother.

"Dad, I know," I told him. "It's just that . . ."

"You're almost eighteen," Mum finished for me, "and you want to see what you can do."

I hadn't thought of it that way, but as soon as she said it, I felt something click into place. I did want to know what I could do. I knew I could lie. I knew I could be good. I wanted to see what else there was, in between those two things.

"Yeah," I said. "Like, you still have to bring me presents and stuff, though."

"The only thing that ever stops your father is the luggage weight limit," Mum said. She and Dad exchanged another look. "We'll start looking into Italy; you spruce up your résumé."

"Awesome," I said. I picked my fork back up and dug into the grocery-store lasagna that Dad usually bought in bulk because it was good for a dinner and then several days of lunches.

Mum and Dad went back to talking about work, and I tuned them out. They tried not to bring too much of it home with them, but the problem was that they were *good* teachers, so they always did anyway. I mostly didn't listen, for self-preservation reasons. I didn't want to know things about other kids or, worse, other teachers. There were definitely things I couldn't be unaware of, however. Mum had several ESL students now, thanks to the two families of Syrian refugees Eganston had sponsored. None of the kids had hit high school yet, so I didn't see them very much, but I appreciated all the work my mother was putting in given her limited resources. Dad, who taught music, had his own funding issues, but he didn't talk about them much because they were super depressing.

By the time I was dragging the crust of my garlic bread around in the remaining sauce and Caesar dressing on my plate, none of us had solved any of our problems, but being able to air them was great. I had convinced them to leave me home alone for at least part of the summer. Now it was time for phase two.

We were at Maddie's house on Friday because her dad was at some fancy travel conference in London and had taken her mother with him because the hotel had an indoor pool. It wasn't anything super organized. Jenny had to work until seven, so we were waiting for her before we started the movie. Maddie's parties—for lack of a better word—were always a bit less chill than hanging out at

Louise's or Mags's, but I understood why. Mags and Louise could host a party for a dozen people on no notice (though Louise would commit a murder at some point, probably) because their families bought groceries in bulk, but Maddie and I had to think about logistics.

"What did your parents say, Jen?" Maddie asked, after making sure that everyone had food, cups, and coasters.

"They're good," I said. It was more of a relief than I let on. I didn't want to be the kid who whined about having to go to Italy if they'd said no.

"That's great!" Louise said. "My parents wouldn't leave me alone with Paul even if they could."

"That's because Paul would force you to murder him," I said. "I don't have that problem."

"Still," Mags said. "A whole house to yourself. Think of the possibilities."

I was about 90 percent sure she was being sarcastic.

"Louise," I said, "I think you should apply for the Young Company, too."

"I have a job at the pool," Louise said. She looked at Maddie. "I mean, not officially, but they're kind of expecting me to come back."

"If the Lions Club is relying on you coming back to open for the summer, they need to rework their business model," Maddie said. "Don't get me wrong, I'll miss you, but I think Jen has a point."

"Different kids," Mags agreed. "Less sunscreen."

"But still good work experience," I said. "Plus I think it'll be fun."

We heard the door downstairs crash open as Jenny came in with a little more gusto than was actually needed so that we'd know she was here.

"We're upstairs!" bellowed Maddie. "There's popcorn next to the microwave!"

We could hear Jenny walking around in the kitchen.

"It's good that we live in a small town," Louise said. "Can you imagine if that was, like, a serial killer?"

I looked out the window and saw Jenny's car parked on the street.

"Well, if it is, they've already stolen her car," I said. "So it's either going to be Jenny with a bowl of popcorn, or we're going to have to avenge her."

It was Jenny, obviously, but we watched some weird nineties horror movie that Maddie's mum had on DVD. Several major plot issues would have been solved immediately if cell phones had been more commonplace, but it was still jumpy in all the right places.

When the movie was over, Louise said she'd drive Mags home so no one had to come and get her. I got in the car with Jenny, because we had a chemistry lab to write up and neither of us wanted to do it over the phone. Maddie pretended that the movie hadn't spooked her, but I knew she'd triple-check all the doors and windows after we left.

"Are you going to be okay?" I asked. I hated leaving her like this, even if we'd all agreed on the movie selection.

"Yeah," she said. "I know it's stupid."

"Can't argue with fight or flight!" Jenny said. "Well, I mean, you can, but not for the first couple of seconds."

We expect girls to come down on the flight side, or usually the much more common freeze side, which isn't even part of the expression. We don't talk about the fight part much. But I guess now I knew where I stood, if lying was fighting.

Jenny's house was noisy, considering it was ten on a Friday

night, but her mum had to get up early to open the store, so we corralled the siblings into the den to keep the house as quiet as possible until we convinced them to go to bed. When we woke up, it was to French toast under a heat lamp in the kitchen, a list of chores on the table, and Constable Jake Postma knocking on the front door.

22.
Jen Dalrymple

Jenny sent her siblings back upstairs before she opened the old wooden door.

"Your mother is fine," Constable Postma started, in full older-brother mode. Jenny relaxed ever so slightly when she realized her mother was okay. He had to speak loudly for us to hear him through the glass of the storm door, but so far Jenny was making no move to let him in.

"Why are you here, then?" Jenny asked.

"You manager said you closed last night at the grocery?" He phrased it as a question instead of a fact, but Jenny didn't answer him. "I just need to know if you sold cigarettes to anyone you didn't know while you were working."

Eganston had had its own police department once. There had been four officers. When they were taken over by the OPP, we started getting cops who were from out of town. Jake was pretty much the only local, but I didn't know if that made it better or worse. Mum and Dad had liked him. Or at least, they hadn't disliked him enough that he was ever in the group of students who were topics of conversation at the dinner table.

"No," Jenny said, handing over one word with obvious reluctance.

"Are you sure?" Postma asked. "You didn't sell Player's Light to someone?"

Jenny looked a bit insulted, and I could tell she was only barely holding herself back from telling him who in Eganston smoked Player's Light and how frequently they came into the store.

"I am sure," she said. She leaned on the wooden door, clearly wanting to close it. We'd been brought up to be polite, but Jenny wasn't about to overextend herself for a police officer, even one she knew.

"Thank you, Jenny," Constable Postma said. "I'll let you get back to your morning. Take care while your mum's at work, okay?"

He turned, missing Jenny's epic eye roll, and she had the door shut and bolted before he was off the steps. We watched him leave through the living room curtains, the squad car pulling lazily out onto the road because there was no traffic at this time of the morning.

"What the fuck was that?" Jenny asked, mostly to no one, so I didn't think too hard about my answer.

"At least Mrs. Ketterly didn't give him your number," I said. The woman who owned the grocery store was trusting in the way that older people are, but not *that* trusting, thankfully. "He had to drive all the way out here."

"Ugh," Jenny said. "I don't want him to have my number."

"Can we come down now?" Adah yelled from upstairs. "I'm starving."

"Yes!" Jenny shouted back. "Make sure Dottie has socks. The kitchen floor is freezing."

We ate the French toast and pretended that it was a normal Saturday. None of the kids asked questions, possibly because

Jenny's face was a storm cloud, and after a small argument about the dishes—it was clearly Dottie's name on the chore list—we went back upstairs to do our homework.

"Do you want to talk about it?" I asked as we got to Jenny's room.

"No," she said. Then she sighed. "I get that there's crime and stuff, but I don't like that people can just come talk to me."

"He's definitely supposed to make sure your mother is present," I said. "He probably thinks he's doing you both a favour by not asking you to come down to the station."

The station was twenty-five minutes away in Goderich.

"Now I'm going to spend the rest of the day thinking about cigarettes," Jenny said. "It was dead last night. Definitely no one from out of town. And only like four people bought cigarettes at all."

"Well, if the constable needs anything else, tell him to call your mother," I said. "The store's number and hours are on Google Maps."

"Let's just get to work," Jenny said.

It only took a couple of hours to write up the lab. Mr. Rogman liked us to do labs by hand and insisted on neat writing or printing. Jenny didn't talk about anything other than homework until we were done, but by the time we went downstairs for a snack, she was back to her normal self. I genuinely thought that would be the end of it, but when we got to school on Monday morning, the whole building was buzzing with rumours.

It was Dahlia who told us what was probably the closest to the truth. Her mother worked at the hospital, same as Louise's, but where Louise's mum only worked there part-time and had to move around to see patients, Dahlia's worked at the desk. Right next to the dispatch for Fire and Emergency.

"They found a dead body in the Abbots' driveway," she said. It had been easier than I'd thought to add a sixth person to our group. We didn't do it all the time, and it was definitely different than it was with Mags and Aaron, but it was still workable. "A decapitated dead body."

"That's disgusting," Mags said.

"Why did Jake come talk to *me*?" Jenny asked.

"There was a pack of cigarettes in the shirt pocket," Dahlia said. "One missing."

Jenny wasn't speechless very often, but this did the trick.

"They thought Jenny was the last person to see him alive?" Maddie said, a whisper turning to a squeak by the end of the question.

The bell rang before Dahlia could tell us anything else. Dahlia gave my hand a quick squeeze before she left. We were still working on that part.

Eganston prides itself on being a nice small town, but the truth is a little bit darker. Meth and other drug scams from the cities reach out to rural areas as a kind of pyramid scheme. The bosses use local kids they don't care about to break into garages for bikes and chain saws to test police reaction times, and then it goes all the way up through the hierarchy of criminals to the actual kingpins who live hours away and don't give a shit. There had been a drive-by shooting when we were in kindergarten, and gunmen had shot the wrong house. Every single one of the people in these instances had been super, super white, but that didn't stop locals from clutching their pearls every time a nonwhite family came to town. Sure, there were only a few of them, but that didn't stop the idiots.

That side of Eganston was something I saw a bit more of than my friends did. Louise's mother was bound by medical confidentiality, and while everyone else had access to gossip, my parents saw things that none of the other parents did. And they had to teach nine-year-olds what human trafficking might look like, which was not something anyone over the age of forty would ever admit existed in their little haven.

"Do you think they'll catch whoever did it?" Louise asked as we made our way to drama.

"I don't think we'll ever find out," I told her. "It's going to be settled in Mississauga, and Eganston will be a footnote in someone's report."

The drama room had a special kind of quiet to it, because it was soundproofed and painted black and there were curtains around the stage mock-up. It had always felt like a little cave, a place where we could build whatever we wanted. That was still true, but I wanted to build more. I wanted to get out of this room, out of this school, out of this town, and take what I'd learned with me. I was a middle-class white girl, and certain things were always going to be easy for me. If my town was going to gasp and whisper about the changing demographics, using me as an example of a thing that needed protecting, then I was going to fight back.

And that was it. That was Maddie's good girl hypothesis applied to my specific set of variables. The conclusion was the same: Mr. Kreskin had nodded and accepted my story as the truth. Constable Postma hadn't cared that I was standing right there while he conducted an investigation I had no part in. I was reliable. Trustworthy. And moreover, I was something they wanted to protect.

Once I had that figured out, deciding on my birthday wish was a piece of cake. I had a while yet to plan, so I wasn't going to say anything to the others, but now I knew what I was looking for. I didn't just want an injustice that I could correct. I wanted an injustice that I could correct *because* of what I was. I wanted to take that power and use it for something good, instead of letting it be directed for me. I wanted to make things better, not for "the good old days"—because they hadn't been—but for the days to come. There wasn't a tonne of opportunity for that in Eganston, but there would be when I got out into the world, and this was an excellent place to practice, because there was so much here that I could control. I would still have to be careful, and I would still have to make sure I covered all of the bases, but there was a whole world out there that wanted to make my path easier, and I was going to let it.

It was never going to be flight and it was never going to be freeze, but they didn't have to know that until after I'd kicked them in the nuts.

23.
Jen Dalrymple

There is a pattern to absolutely everything in a small town, if you know how to look for it. That spring, it warmed up early, and as soon as it was nice enough for the kids to start riding their bikes to school again, I went looking for a pattern.

Eganston Elementary School was small, and almost every grade had a Syrian student. By the end of the second year after they came to town, the kids could communicate fluently, and because my mum had bent over backwards to include Syrian culture in the curriculum as much as she could, most of the white kids knew basic greetings in Arabic, what Ramadan meant, and how to turn chickpeas into hummus.

The Syrian kids also all had bikes. That's what the elementary school had given as their gift when the families moved to town—to make the kids part of the community. Seven kids, seven bikes, each one slightly bigger than the kid needed, because they'd arrived in January.

The Syrian kids rode their bikes a lot. Mum said they'd all had bikes before they came here, and they were thrilled to have new ones. They wore their helmets and rode on the right side of the street, stopping at every stop sign and walking their bikes if they crossed at the lights, which the sign said to do and no one ever actually did.

For the most part, no one hassled them.

Of course, they weren't the only kids with bicycles, and there was a weird phenomenon when a large group of teenage boys had bikes. They got brave enough to pursue what they thought were weak targets. They still didn't go after their new neighbours directly, but they did always seem to be at the park if one of the families was having a picnic or something, circling like sharks. Or they rode up and down the street if a family was out for a walk. There had been enough violence against people of colour on the news that I was dead set against it happening here. I just didn't know how I could stop it until after Constable Postma knocked on Jenny's door.

As spring progressed and more of the bikes came out, I made coded notes about where the boys went and what they did. It was harmless stuff—or at least that's what an adult would say. But I could feel it, the potential for danger in the air. They were just a little bit too close. A little bit too interested. A little bit too . . . much. And they were all in high school, older than the Syrian kids. All it would take was one of them getting an idea, and we'd have a bunch of ignorant mini white supremacists on our hands, and I knew that no one in Eganston would be able to deal with that.

This was not my only project. In addition to homework and band stuff, Dahlia, and planning for the summer, Louise and I had both been hired by the Young Company, and I needed to update my first aid certificate. I talked Maddie into coming with me to those classes. Most critically, I needed to decide what I was going to do in the fall. Universities would be sending acceptances starting soon, at the end of March, and even though I knew where I didn't want to go, I didn't have anything more specific than that. It got to the point where I found myself staring at the board outside the guidance office contemplating tree planting before I had a moment of clarity.

University was going to be a bigger bubble than Eganston was, but it was still a tightly defined sort of place. You had to have money to go there, or the ability to convince someone that you were reliable enough to give money to, and that tended to create a predictable social climate. If I was going to do something that only privileged kids could do, I wanted there to be a *chance* that it would teach me how to unpack something.

"Maddie," I said. "I think we should do Katimavik next year instead of going right to university."

I was at her house, and we were pulling apart newspapers for World Issues. We had to record and file—which was academic language for "scrapbook"—everything about our assigned countries, so we had decided to split subscriptions to the three actual print newspapers, even though the *National Post* was usually pretty vomit inducing. Jenny and Mags were in on it, too, but they were busy, so we were pulling their articles for them.

"What?" said Maddie. "The house-building thing?"

"It's not houses," I said. "It's a six-month work placement, usually in the north. They focus on Reconciliation now."

I watched Maddie try to process it. I had definitely surprised her.

"Look, there's no guarantee we both get accepted, and there's absolutely no guarantee we end up in the same place, but . . ." I trailed off for a moment. "I just think it would be good."

"Your parents would let you defer for a year?" Maddie asked.

"My parents are still mad that OACs were eliminated," I told her. "If I wanted to spend a fifth year here, they'd understand. I think they'd be pleased I'm taking more time before declaring a major. Plus I'm only going to have one summer of work experience and some volunteering. My résumé is really thin."

"I like the idea of doing something for Reconciliation instead of just reading about it," Maddie said. "Are they, like, good at it?"

"Well, obviously their website is biased," I said. "But I think so."

Maddie thought about it for a few minutes, still scanning the papers in front of her. I wasn't going to rush her. I didn't know why I was so keen to barrel towards change, and I certainly wasn't going to force anyone to come with me. I just wanted to. A lot.

"All right," she said, nodding. "I'll do the application, at least."

"Awesome," I said. "I think we have a good shot."

"What about the others?" Maddie asked. She always tended to think of the group, and I thought of us as individuals. Each had its strength, and together, it made us even more effective.

"Louise and Mags don't have time," I said. "And Jenny doesn't have time for a different reason."

"That's probably true," Maddie said. She laughed. "It literally never would have occurred to me, Jen, and now I can't stop thinking about how it's kind of perfect."

"I was the same," I said. "I just happened to look at the corkboard outside the guidance office while I was in the right mood."

We finished with the articles, sorting the folders for Mags and Jenny, and then went to the Katimavik website. The application seemed pretty straightforward, if painfully earnest, but earnest was something I could conjure up. It helped that I actually thought the work they were doing was a good idea. I just didn't tend to be all that effusive. We printed off the forms so we could practice our answers before submitting them, and spent the afternoon trying to find the exact tone that would get us in, while not making us look like lunatics.

"You've picked your birthday wish already," Maddie said.

She caught me so off guard that I nodded before I thought about what answer I wanted to give her. Then I decided to try putting my hesitation into words.

"It's a lot of work," I said. "I'm trying to figure it out so that when I tell everyone, we don't have to do too much planning. It's a bit time sensitive."

"We're supposed to do this together," Maddie said. "That was the whole point."

"Yeah, but we keep getting more public," I said. "And this one is very public. So I wanted to make sure I was prepared."

"Mr. Kreskin really freaked you out, didn't he?" Maddie asked.

"Not enough to give up," I said. "Or chicken out, or tell on us. But enough that I wanted to consider my options. Does that make sense?"

"Yes," Maddie said. "I almost peed my pants, and you saved me, so as far as I'm concerned, you can take all the time you want."

It was the first time we'd ever talked about that day without the others present. It was nice to know she'd been as scared as I was, and as surprised that we'd pulled it off. Maddie tended to be so confident in the right side winning that she assumed more good in the world than there was. It was one of my favourite things about her, and it gave her a bullheaded approach that I appreciated, but that time it had almost been too much.

"Well, I've got a couple of months," I said. "And plenty to do in the meantime."

"How's the other thing going?" Maddie asked. She was the

only person I'd told about the "other thing," because I wanted to make sure it wasn't a completely stupid idea. Maddie, naturally, had been immediately onside as soon as I'd explained it, and hadn't breathed a word since.

"It's fine," I said. "I'm almost done. Then we just have to see how it comes together. I don't think it'll embarrass Jenny. Or at least, I hope not."

I really, really hoped not.

"It won't," Maddie said. "I mean, she might punch you a little bit for making her feel feelings in public, but I think she'll get it."

My phone buzzed, a text indicating that my parents were on their way home from school. It was almost six, so I packed my folder in my backpack, said good-bye to Maddie's mother, who had just come through the door, and headed home. I didn't even bother to do up my coat, though it was still a bit chilly.

By the time Mum and Dad got in, I had a frozen baked mac and cheese in the oven. I knew that it wasn't really supposed to be a meal, but it was my favourite comfort food, and so sometimes we all pretended that it was. Dad was buzzing because he and Mr. Carter had set up more details of the Italy trip, which explained why Maddie's dad hadn't been home yet when I left her house. Travel agents don't work overtime, but neighbours do. Dad sounded so excited while he described the house that he'd managed to book that it made me smile, too.

"And it's close to some kind of chocolate festival," Dad finished up, "so finding something to bring home for you will not be a problem."

"That sounds perfect," I said. Summer was falling into place all around us.

"Yeah," Dad said. "I think we'll be fine."

Now I only had to make sure that when they came home, it would be to a daughter who still didn't have a criminal record, and a town that might be just a little bit better than it had been when they left.

That's what friends are for.

24.
Jen Dalrymple

The last week of April, when Jenny and I were called into the office, I had no idea what to expect. We were both in chemistry when it happened, so we walked down together. Jenny was as confused as I was, but it wasn't a long enough walk for us to have much of a discussion about it.

Mrs. Kelly was absolutely beaming as she escorted us down the hall of the admin office, away from her desk and towards one of the meeting rooms. There were three strangers waiting for us, one of them with a recording device and a fancy-looking microphone. The other two stood up to introduce themselves.

"Hello, girls," the shorter woman said. "My name is Alice, I'm one of the managers at the Mill on the Bend. This is my colleague Becky, who is one of our clothing buyers. The gentleman with the microphone is Scott from CKNX."

I let myself smile as we all shook hands, but tried to keep my reaction small. Now I knew what we were all doing here, but I wanted it to be a surprise for Jenny for as long as possible.

"So," Becky said. "As you know, the Mill on the Bend holds a competition every year, where members of the community can nominate young people who they feel deserve an extra-special gift for their prom: an outfit they can wear to the dance. This year we

had something happen that had never happened before, and we
wanted to share it with both of you."

Now I was back to being confused. Surely there hadn't been
that much that was weird about the essay I'd submitted. I sneaked
a look at Jenny. She looked guarded.

"I'm going to read the first one," Alice said. She cleared her
throat and began. " 'I don't know when I noticed, or how. It must
have been about grade four, and she must have worn something I
recognized, and that helped me put the pieces together.' "

Hearing my words read out loud was strange, but not as strange
as the expression on Jenny's face. This was clearly not what she'd
been expecting to hear.

" 'For years, my mother has donated my used clothes to a local
thrift shop,' " Alice continued. " 'And for years, my friend's mother
has bought them. I'm sure you guys remember what high school
was like, so I have never said anything about it. It actually became
kind of fun for me, like, when I went shopping, I would pick things
I thought she'd like.' "

I thought Mrs. Kelly's face might actually split in two from
how widely she was smiling. It was a bit embarrassing.

" 'But that's not going to work for a prom dress,' " Alice read.
" 'We're going to need one at the same time. I want Jenny Hoernig
to have a dress for prom that no one else has worn, that's just for
her. She's worked insanely hard through school, and she's a really
good friend. And I want her to have a new dress.' "

Jenny grabbed my hand, squeezing so hard I worried she might
break my fingers before she relaxed a bit. When I looked at her
face, I realized she was trying not to cry. I was instantly worried
that I'd hurt her feelings, outing her situation like this. Except in

my notes on the essay, I'd specifically said *not* to reveal the name in public. And the radio guy was here.

"Jen did ask for anonymity," Becky said. "But we wanted you both to hear this."

Alice picked up a second piece of paper and cleared her throat again. This time it sounded suspiciously harder.

" 'My family has never been hungry and we've never been cold, but we don't always get new stuff,' " she read. " 'My mum buys a lot of our clothes at the thrift store, and a lot of the clothes she buys for me used to be owned by one of my best friends.' "

My whole mind went entirely blank. Suddenly I was the one squeezing Jenny's hand. She'd known. For years.

" 'She's never said anything, but I think she knows, because in grade five or so, she started buying clothes I like,' " Alice continued. " 'Sometimes she'd even take me shopping with her and ask my opinion on stuff.' "

I guess I hadn't been as subtle as I thought. Maybe I won't work for CSIS after all.

" 'We're coming up on prom, and I'm submitting Jen Dalrymple's name for your contest, because I want her to pick a dress that's just for her,' " Alice said. " 'I don't want her to have to think about what colours look good on me, or what I said about recent styles. You'll probably have to tell her why she's won, if she does, and then she'll know that I'm onto her, but I really do think that she deserves it.' "

Alice set the second letter down on the table and smiled at us beatifically.

"You both win, obviously," Becky said, cutting the tension slightly. "We went through about a box of Kleenex setting this up with your guidance counsellor. You girls are exactly what we had in mind when we started this contest a few years ago. I can't wait to take you both shopping."

I had no idea what to say. I had hoped that Jenny would be picked, but I had no idea that she'd submitted an entry of her own. From the expression on her face, it was clear she had the same feelings about me.

"I understand if you two don't want to talk about it," Alice said. "But if you do, we would love to share your stories. Obviously it's great marketing for us, but I also think that people like hearing about good stuff."

I looked at Jenny. As far as I was concerned, it was entirely up to her. Her secret was much bigger than mine, and she still had three younger siblings to consider.

"I'm okay talking about it," Jenny said. "Just don't record any part where we're crying?"

At that, Mrs. Kelly started laughing, and it quickly spread through the room. Even Scott from CKNX laughed.

"I'll leave you to it, then," Mrs. Kelly said. "Just make sure to wrap it up in time to go get your books. I'm very proud of you girls. You are exactly what we hope our students grow into."

I very much did not make eye contact with Jenny, because I knew that she was wondering the same thing I was. I doubted Mrs. Kelly would feel the same way if she knew who was to blame for the basketball uniforms. Or the etiquette lessons that Mags's uncle was still coming to the school to teach. Or what had happened to Trevor Harrow.

Or what I was going to do next.

Being a good girl could get you pretty far. It could all come crashing down at any moment, but if you were careful, people would go out of their way to reward you for being good and kind and predictable. I was fully prepared to take advantage of them. I wanted Jenny to have a nice dress, and I certainly wasn't going to turn down a free one, either. But I was going to use that reputation as much as possible. It didn't do me any good lying around. Amelia Chaser had proved that. So had Isobel and Elizabeth. Even Char had lost their credibility for being their real self. If my reputation wasn't permanent, I was going to make the best of it while it lasted.

Mrs. Kelly left us with the Mill ladies and Scott from CKNX. First we set a date and time for when we were going to go shopping. After we'd worked that out, we answered a few questions, mostly managing to keep it together, and they turned us loose about five minutes before the bell was going to ring. Instead of heading for the main stairs—the quickest way back to the chemistry room—Jen took my hand and pulled me towards the stairs at the far end of the hall. Part of the school had been taken over by a day care and school board technology centre, and since there were no classrooms, the stairs were very rarely used. This meant that if we stopped on the landing, no one would be able to see us.

"I cannot believe you did that," Jenny said, quietly because the stairwells echoed quite a bit.

"I can't believe *you* did!" I replied. It was still taking everything I had not to burst into hysterical laughter. I refused to cry about this. It was way too good. "And I can't believe you knew the whole time."

"Not the whole time," Jenny said. "Just after your mum remarried."

We hadn't talked about it for years, mostly because I didn't know how, but I knew exactly what she meant. When I found out I was getting a dad—and one I already liked, at that—I was over the moon. In a lot of ways, I still was. Jenny never got that, and I was always afraid she'd feel like I had left her behind. It wasn't pity or even charity that had made me take such good care of my clothes. It was that I would have done absolutely anything to make her even a fraction as happy as I was.

"I love you," I said, because it was really the only thing I could think of. I hadn't even dreamed of saying it to Dahlia yet, because it would mean something else if I did, but saying it to Jenny was as easy as breathing.

"I love you, too," Jenny said. "We'd better get back. If Mags and Maddie have to carry our books, you know they'll mix them up on purpose."

"They'd better not," I said. "Or we won't be their dates to prom."

"Oh man, you totally have to tell Louise," Jenny said. "She's going to be furious that she has to come."

"I'll tell her she can host the after-party," I said. "And that only the five of us will be there."

"Not seven?" Jenny asked. "Though maybe Aaron doesn't want to go through it all again."

I blinked at her. Holy shit, I was going to have to ask a girl to prom.

Jenny laughed so hard I almost had to carry her back to the chemistry classroom.

25.
Jen Dalrymple

When I blew out the candles on my birthday cake, I opened my eyes to find everyone looking at me expectantly. It never crossed their minds I wouldn't make a wish, even though it had been months since Louise's and we were all feeling the crunch that came with the end of high school. I don't think Maddie had told them what I had been thinking about, how it was complicated and maybe too much to ask. They all looked hopeful and curious.

"Okay, so this is what I want," I said. "It's not super practical, I don't think? And it's a bit more . . . visible than the other stuff we've done."

"You and Louise won't have juvie records now," Mags reminded us. "It'll be on your permanent record if you're caught."

"Yeah, but I don't think this is a crime," I told her. "It's just annoying."

"Tell us," Jenny said. "I know you've been sitting on it for weeks and you have a fourteen-point plan ready to go."

"It's only six points," I joked. Then I settled back on the couch to explain while Louise cut the cake and passed slices around.

"This isn't a onetime thing," I said. "It might take up most of the summer, actually. And I'm hoping that after we leave, other people will continue."

"That's definitely the opposite of subtle," Maddie said.

Louise sat down beside me and handed over my piece of cake. I took a couple of bites before I kept going, and no one interrupted me, because no one interrupted Louise's death by chocolate cake.

"Okay," I said, reaching for my pop. "You know that horrible 'if you see something, say something' thing that people use to get people they don't like in trouble?"

There were nods all around.

"I want to do that, here in Eganston, but I want to target those gangs of boys that ride their bikes around town in the summer," I said.

"They don't do anything," Mags said.

"They don't do anything *yet*," I told her. "And I never want them to. They circle girls at the pool and they spend way too much time biking up and down the streets the Syrian families live on. It's only a matter of time before they get the wrong TikTok, feel brave, and do something awful."

"So when we see them around, we say something?" Maddie asked. "To who?"

"We call the police," I said. "Not the emergency number, the other one. And we only call them when it's white boys, which is pretty much always."

"What are the police going to do?" Jenny demanded. "Jake Postma still plays hockey with most of their older brothers. And a lot of those cops are strangers. They're more likely to get the people we're trying to help in trouble."

"That's why we need to be careful," I said. "They record all those conversations, so we make sure we're always describing the white kids. We definitely don't call them if the Syrian kids are around. And we always say that *we* are the ones who are uncomfortable."

They all digested it for a moment. I ate three more bites of cake.

"So in this magical world of yours," Louise said, "do the police actually do anything?"

"No," I said. "Well, not anything super concrete. They're going to be in town anyway, and I think they'd be more useful if they were theoretically preventing crime and not handing out speeding tickets."

"What if it makes them all weirdly hypervigilant?" Maddie asked.

"They'll be weirdly hypervigilant about white kids," I said. "They'll think they're protecting nice white girls, and we'll make sure they're focusing on white boys."

"I think I actually like it," Jenny said. We all looked at her in a bit of surprise. I thought Jenny would be the hardest one to convince. "As you said, we're stuck with a revolving door of OPP officers anyway. We might as well use them for something. And you're right about the boys, too. Dottie hasn't even gotten her bike out of the garage yet, and she's usually biking to school the minute the roads are clear."

"It all comes back to what Maddie said about being good girls," I said. "It's not enough for me to use that for defence. I want to use it for offence, too. Eganston is really small and really white, but I don't think it's a terrible place to practice. Whether we're planning to stay here or leave."

"All right," said Louise. Her fingers were twitching like she wanted to make a list. I realized how stressful it must be for her to keep all of this in her head. I was really proud of her. "I think we should start small, though. No more than three calls a week until July."

"Agreed," Mags said. "And we should look at a map of the town and pick places where we will call and places where we won't."

"I think the pool is our best shot," Maddie said. "It keeps everything public and open, and there are a lot of people's daughters there. In bathing suits, no less."

"It would be nice if we were people," Jenny said. "But I guess that's why we're doing this."

I took another bite of cake to cover the rising feeling of gratefulness in my chest. If I wasn't careful, I'd do something expressive, like cry.

"Thank you," I said. "I know this one is weird."

"They've all been weird," Maddie said. "And they've all been different, like us. I think it's natural that we've progressed as we've worked through everyone's birthdays."

"I'm still mad there's no way to put this on my résumé," Louise said. Jenny threw a pillow at her, and Louise managed to dodge without spilling any of her cake on the floor.

"Have you asked Dahlia yet?" Jenny said.

I hadn't been expecting the subject change, and choked a little bit. Everyone turned to look at me. I gaped like a fish.

"Do you want her to ask you?" Mags asked. "Because that's totally understandable."

"I don't know," Jen said. "When I entered the dress contest thingy, I wasn't actually thinking about going to the formal."

"Neither was I," Jenny said. She curled up on the beanbag chair, giggling like a loon. "I still can't believe we both won."

"I can't believe you made Mrs. Kelly cry," Maddie said. "She's so proud of you she hasn't badgered Jenny about her 'postsecondary options' in days."

"Look," said Louise, "just ask her. It doesn't have to be a big deal. Ask her if she's going, ask her if she wants to go with you, and then ask her if she minds also going with us. And you can tell her that Mum and Dad are hosting all of us and our parents for a potluck in the driveshed beforehand, because they are insane and weirdly happy that I'm going at all."

I considered it. When she outlined it so straightforwardly, it seemed entirely doable.

"Oh, and act surprised when Mum gives you the invitations," Louise added. "She spent a long time on them."

"I'm going to go call her right now," I said. "You know, before common sense kicks in and I text her a meme or something."

They were still teasing me when I closed the door to the rumpus room, and stood in the little office at the top of the staircase we rarely used because the loft ladder was more fun. I did actually text first, because I wasn't about to call her randomly. She called back almost immediately, and I answered before I had time to finish thinking my way through what I was about to say.

"Aren't you at your own birthday party right now?" Dahlia said. She was coming to dinner on the night of my actual birthday, so I hoped she didn't feel too left out.

"Yes," I said. "But I wanted to ask you something."

"What is it?" she asked.

I could hardly get the words out, until I made myself follow Louise's script.

"Are you going to the formal?" I asked.

"Oh," she said. "I mean, I guess so? I know it's just a dance with slightly more papier-mâché, but it's probably still fun."

"Right," I said. I took a deep breath. "Do you want to go with me?"

I know you can't actually hear someone smiling over the phone, but it felt like I could actually hear her smiling over the phone.

"Yes," she said. "I would love to go with you."

"Do you mind if the others are there as well?" I asked. "And maybe Aaron Jantzi, too. I don't know what Mags's plan is."

"That sounds like fun," she said. "My other friends are planning something super fancy, and I wasn't entirely keen on it, so it's extra good news for me."

"Awesome," I said. I was pretty sure my grin was maniacal by this point. "Mrs. Jantzi has something planned for dinner, but the only detail I know is that it'll happen in the driveshed, so it's probably not going to be fancy. I am not sure how it'll work around Shabbat, though."

"That actually seems kind of perfect." Dahlia laughed. "And I'll figure it out."

"Or the regionals for track and field," I added. Dahlia was a distance runner who usually made it to provincials.

"That too!" Dahlia said. "I'll let you get back to everyone. I really appreciate you calling to ask. I hadn't worked up the nerve yet."

"They had to talk me into it," I admitted.

"Did Louise make a list?" Dahlia asked.

"Yes," I told her. She laughed again. I liked the sound more every time I heard it.

"Call me tomorrow?" Dahlia said. "I'll be with Grandpa in the morning, but home all afternoon."

"I will," I said. "Have a good night! I'll save you some cake."

For a moment, I wanted to stay in the office forever. It was perfect there, one happy little bubble. But I knew that there was more to come. Some of it would suck, but most of it would be okay. So I opened the door and went back to my party.

SIXTH WISH:

Arson

(OR: MADDIE CARTER'S 18TH BIRTHDAY)

26.
Maddie Carter

We fully expected to spend the summer lounging around, occasionally calling Constable Postma or whoever else was on duty if there were too many boys hanging around at the pool, and generally enjoying one last summer before we went off to university. And we could have, assuming Jen's wish didn't take a bad turn despite the measures we took to prevent that. It would have been very, very easy.

School acceptances continued to roll in. The formal came and went. We all drove to Sarnia to cheer for Dahlia at the regionals for track and field. Emily was back home for the summer, and Mum and Dad were doing their best to give her the freedom she was used to while also still being her parents. All I wanted was to study for exams, find out if our Katimavik applications had been successful, and then start the awkward process of informing my parents that I'd be deferring university for a year.

I wish I wondered what kind of person you had to be to revel in the misery of others. It would be nice to be continually mystified by human cruelty, surprised by the way one person judged another against an arbitrary set of rules and then rubbed their faces in it. But the truth is that I wasn't. I knew exactly what kind of person you had to be. You had to be a nice, upstanding member of the community. The kind of person who volunteered at the hospital and taught kids how to fix tractors. You had to also be the kind of person who looked into their own soul and was so scared by what they saw there that they just *needed* to bring someone else down to their level. And you had to be the kind of person who was willing to put up a billboard a whole year after a girl's decisions stopped being even remotely any of your business.

You had to be Margaret and Jan Pedersen.

"A big fire?" Jenny asked as I crested the top of the ladder and took a seat in the rumpus room. She didn't sound all that surprised.

"I'm honestly not sure how big," I said. "I mean, we have to make sure we keep it contained, and I'm not exactly sure how that works."

"You want to burn down the billboard." Mags didn't say it as a question. Everything from the last year had led us to this. "You'd have to wait until after they bring the beans in, or the whole field would go up. And it's close to the Chasers' house, and I'm assuming you don't want to burn that down."

"No," I said. "Just the sign."

Louise sank back into one of the beanbag chairs. Jen was looking thoughtful.

"I figured you'd want to make another wish," Louise said. "Which is why I asked. I guess escalation shouldn't be a huge surprise."

"Is it really escalation?" Jen asked. "I mean, we've ruined a dude's life. He was an asshole, but still."

"We can argue comparative morals later," Jenny said. "Right now we have to talk about logistics."

Louise launched herself out of the chair and went over to the desk where the 4-H club kept the arts and crafts supplies that the younger kids used. She got a piece of paper and a marker, and then came back to sit at the coffee table.

"I'll destroy it when we're done," she said. "But I need to see all of this to understand it."

No one voiced any protest. We all agreed with her. We'd done big things and we'd done noticeable things, but fire was somehow a completely different level. We couldn't leave anything to chance, and we all trusted Louise to take care of any paper trail she might leave while she was crystalizing the details.

"First thing is timing," Jenny said. "Mags is right about the beans. So this means we'll do it at the end of August. And obviously at night, right?"

"Yes," Louise said. "The road isn't busy, so darkness is good cover. We won't be able to use flashlights or anything, though, because if someone sees a light, there won't be anything else to pass it off as."

"Right," Mags said. "We'll have to be careful of tracks, though hopefully the dirt will be kind of dry. Tire treads, too."

"Accelerant?" Jen asked.

"It'll have to be gasoline," I said. "But we'll buy it in cash, somewhere like Goderich or even London."

"The hard part is going to be scoping out the road," Louise said. "We'll have to be out there in daylight to figure out where the best entry and exit points are so we can find them in the dark."

"The conservation area backs onto that road," Mags said. "There's four little parking lots, I think? At least two on the concession we need."

"I'll take care of that part," I said. It would be the most exposed roll of the preparation, and the most likely to be remembered by a witness. "I'll have access to the car, and I don't mind driving on gravel. I can say that I want to get used to more outside time before I go to Katimavik."

"You'll have to use all the lots," Jenny pointed out. "Sort of randomly. And you hate hiking."

"I'll figure something out," I said. I looked around the room at everyone. "This one's different."

I wasn't entirely sure they'd know what I meant. Before, the things we'd done had been almost invisible. Things to be shrugged off as strange coincidences, or a one-off event in the case of the basketball jerseys. A fire was something that people in Eganston would talk about for years, especially one that was without question set deliberately.

"Yeah," Mags said. "But I want to do it."

This was the first Sunday in months that Mags had been to church with her family. She'd gone to witness Amelia, to be the one reassuring smile when it came time to exchange the peace, but she was still angry about it.

"Me too," Jenny said. "If there's no pushback, nothing will ever change."

"It's worse than that," Jen said. "If there's no pushback, they'll assume people agree with them and approve of what they're doing."

"Anything missing?" Louise had been writing things down as we spoke. She turned the paper around so that I could read it.

"There's bound to be something unpredictable," I said. "Like, what if someone hires worm pickers, or something like that?"

Louise added "something unpredictable" to the list. She reached over for the huge cup of Coke she had been sipping out of. The cup was about half full, so when she started shredding up the paper, there was space for her to shove it in. We watched, Jenny reaching over to pour in some of her pop when the paper soaked up all the Coke.

"Thanks, everyone," I said. "I still don't know why this feels so important."

It had never been vengeance, exactly. That was probably the easiest word to explain, but maybe the better one was "resistance." Like Jen said, everything we did gave evidence that we did not approve of how things were done. Even if it felt petty and small, it was still something.

"It's important because it's you," Mags said. "Because it's home. Because some of us want to leave and some of us don't, but in both cases, what happens here matters."

Louise finished with the mess she was making of her list, and went to throw it out. Some went in the regular garbage, some in the office garbage—wrapped in Kleenex—and some she even flushed down the toilet. Then she went to the fridge and got my birthday cake out. She set it on the counter and pressed the candles into the icing, three rows of six. She picked up the lighter, and then passed it over to me.

"I know it's not exactly traditional," she said. "But I think it's fitting."

I flicked the lighter on and held it carefully to the wicks. By the time I got to the last one, the first was dripping wax onto the top of the cake, but no one rushed me while I set the lighter down and pulled myself together. We looked at each other across the flames, a little solemn for a birthday party, but we all knew why. Louise squeezed my hand and Mags nodded at me. I closed my eyes and leaned forwards to blow out the candles.

———————

The Londsett Marsh wasn't particularly exciting as far as conservation areas went. It was municipal, so it wasn't even crown land. Aside from a pair of bald eagles that had nested here for one summer half a decade ago, there weren't any notable animals. You could see deer and maybe a muskrat or two, but those were just as easily viewable from any farmhouse window.

What the marsh did have was a lot of bird boxes. They were built by shop classes at both ECSS and the public Catholic high school, though the funding for ECSS woodworking had long since dried up. New boxes were added every season, but most of the action was in the older boxes, because that's where the established birds would make their nests. It was still only home for things like red-winged blackbirds and chickadees, but there were a lot of them, and so that's what people came to see.

I realized the advantages of bird watching very quickly. Even though getting Constable Postma's attention was the last thing I wanted, his book had been surprisingly useful. Looking at birds meant less hiking, which I was not super into as an excuse to be out here. It also gave me a reason to be at the marsh at various times of day, particularly in the evening, when the birds were coming home. Most importantly, it provided the perfect excuse to be out here with binoculars, and if sometimes they were trained on the Pedersen farmhouse instead of seeking out elusive woodpeckers, well, there usually weren't too many people around to notice.

Also, it turned out that birds were sort of neat.

We still had the last few weeks of school to get through, of course, but having a plan always made me feel better. Our teachers had more or less given up on actual classwork, and we split our time between exam prep and messing around. Jenny got into

Western and Fanshaw but didn't want to talk about it, so none of us pressed, and the rest of us all had our first choices. Jen and I were deferring because we had been accepted into Katimavik. We were being sent to opposite ends of the country, but it was still exciting. My parents had been pretty thrilled about it, in the end, which was nice.

It was finally going to happen. The thing that we'd resisted since nursery school, when the five of us banded together for the first time. We were going to split up. And yes, there were phones and the internet, but it was never going to be the same again. I was excited and a little bit scared, but mostly I felt like I had unfinished business. And I wasn't talking about my exams.

We had something else to take care of first.

27.
Maddie Carter

The third week of July, a concerned parent wrote an anonymous letter to the local paper. This was not completely unheard of, but it did take some effort to pull off when most submissions came online. I wondered if the sender had paid for a stamp or if they'd just dropped it through the mail slot one evening when the office was closed. The *Record* published it in the news section instead of the opinion section because it was a slow week, and because the opinion section was completely filled up by people arguing about if we needed a second stoplight (technically a crosswalk). It might have gone unnoticed due to incredibly low readership, but the library was doing a local news reading program with their teen group that summer, and so a bunch of them read it the day the paper came out.

The concern was that the police, specifically Constable Postma because he was the most recognizable, were being called to the swimming pool too frequently. After all, the boys had just as much a right to be there as anyone else. Never mind that they traveled in a leering pack and almost always targeted kids who were by themselves or with one other friend. I was supposed to be watching kids swimming, so I didn't always see it when Postma was there, but by the third week of July, I figured it was something close to every other day. That still wasn't every time the boys showed up.

The mother, because it was so obviously one of the boys' mothers, worried that not only was her sweet boy getting a complex about being confronted by an armed officer so frequently, it was a misuse of local resources. Eganston only had one police officer on patrol in town at any given time, though of course more could be brought in if they were required. Constable Postma did not belong at the pool. He belonged elsewhere in town, solving actual crime.

"Has Constable Postma ever solved a crime in his life?" Jenny asked dismissively. "Like, do speeding tickets count?"

She rolled up the newspaper and threw it at Mags so she could put it in the bonfire. It was too hot for a fire, but Mags's little sisters had wanted s'mores, and we'd been forcibly evicted from the kitchens of both houses. The girls had run off, covered in sugar, to go brag about the treat while presumably attracting every mosquito in the county. Which was fine with me, because I hated mosquito bites.

"That's not really the point," Jen said. She poked the fire with a marshmallow spike, burning off the remaining gooeyness so she could start over on the next one. "I'm more worried that we're calling too frequently."

"I've only called twice," I said. Everyone looked at me, and I shrugged. I rummaged through the basket Mags's grandma had sent outside with us, hoping to find hot dogs. "The first week of summer vacation, I called the Wednesday evening and the Sunday afternoon."

"I called from my phone once, and I used Dottie's phone once," Jenny said. She was eating the chocolate plain, and Louise was pointedly ignoring her. "But that's it."

"I called when they were using the wheelchair ramps at town hall as a skate park," Louise said. She passed me one of the multipronged skewers so I could cook my hot dog without dropping it. "The mayor was yelling at them when Jake showed up because the actual skate park is literally two blocks away."

"So who else is calling?" Mags said. Free of younger siblings, she leaned back in her lawn chair and looked up at the darkening sky.

None of us knew the answer, but the next week there were two letters to the editor, both written as responses. Again, they were printed in the news section (the crosswalk debate raged on hotly in opinion), but this time they were closer to the front of the paper, and the headlines were marginally bigger. Clearly someone thought this was getting interesting.

The first letter was anonymous, asking the "concerned parent" what crimes exactly they thought Constable Postma should be looking at if there were kids in the park who were worried enough about their safety to call him. The writer argued that Postma would, at the very least, be providing a good example for the boys, and literally used the expression "an ounce of prevention is worth a pound of cure."

The second letter was not anonymous. It was from Alice Mac-Gregor, a fourteen-year-old girl who had been in youth group with Mags. Her family was well-known in town because they were all athletes outside of school. Her brother Davy played broomball, two of her cousins curled at the provincial level, and her younger sisters comprised approximately half the girls' hockey program in their age group. Alice was a swimmer, so she was at the pool almost as much as I was. She was too young to have a lifeguard job yet, but it was only a matter of time, and meanwhile, she was on the swim team. Alice admitted to calling Postma twice herself, because the boys made her nervous and said rude things to her about her bathing suit in front of her younger sisters.

"Holy shit," Jen said.

We hadn't been expecting a follow-up in the paper, so we hadn't planned a get-together for that afternoon. Jenny had texted everyone after picking Dottie up from the library, where she and the rest of the teen group had once again been amongst the first to read the news. My parents were in London, so everyone came to my house as they finished their shifts at work. I meant to order a pizza, but it was so hot we ended up just taking every popsicle we could find and heading out to the backyard.

We inflated my old kiddie pool and filled it with all the ice cubes from the freezer. It wasn't a lot, and it melted pretty fast, but we could sit in a circle around the pool and at least keep our feet at a reasonable temperature. Jen had brought a cooler of ice from her house, but we were using it for drinks and to hold off the sticky end the popsicles were headed for. It was after six, but the humidity didn't show any signs of breaking.

"The best part is that everyone knows Alice is on the swim team," Jenny said. "They literally did a feature with a picture of her at the beginning of summer. Everyone knows what her bathing suit looks like."

"Not to mention some random adult took her side," I said. "Probably without knowing it, but still."

I wondered if those were the only two letters the paper had received, or if those were just the two that were chosen. I wondered what would happen next week when the paper came out. I wondered if readership would go up, however briefly, like it had the time a reporter covered all the fall fair events over the course of two months and accidentally printed Mrs. Phillips's secret chicken recipe.

"How's the stakeout going?" Louise asked.

We hadn't talked that much about the fire since my birthday, aside from my brief run-in with Constable Postma at the very beginning. There was no point in gathering the materials this far out, so there wasn't much to do. We had a vague idea of what we'd need and a rough concept of the timeline, but planning anything too much seemed like a good way to get caught. Or worry ourselves silly. It seemed best to leave it alone until circumstances were ready.

"Pretty quiet," I said. "The Chasers go up to their cottage a lot, and the Pedersens just do normal farm stuff. I did see a cedar waxwing this week, though. That was cool."

Jenny looked at me like I was off my gourd, but didn't say anything.

"Any other people?" Mags asked.

"Well," I said. "There are a few other bird watchers. There's a club, apparently. I told them I wasn't really interested in joining since I was going to school in the fall. They might all be octogenarians."

The club was actually pretty chill, and not as old as I joked, though they were definitely all in the retirement age bracket. In the winter, one of their husbands used a snowmobile to make a ski trail through the old sugar bush for them so they could go cross-country skiing without having to break the snow. It was only kind of trespassing. In the summer they just wandered around looking for birds. They'd all lived in Eganston for years, and they'd tried having a book club, but it wasn't like they couldn't bring their snacks with them into the woods. I didn't for a moment imagine that the five of us would turn out like them, but it was nice to know that grown-ups still did unconventional things just for the sake of being together and getting out of the house.

"They don't think it's weird that you're out there by yourself?" Louise asked. I think she still felt bad about leaving me by myself at the pool, even though I had told her it was fine. I even meant it. I missed her, of course, but I wasn't insulted about it, or upset.

"No," I said. "I think they have all accepted a certain level of weird."

Jenny got a lime popsicle out of the cooler, deftly broke it in half, opened the package, and handed the other stick to Mags.

"Are there any—" Jen began, and then caught the banana popsicle that Jenny had already thrown at her head. "Thanks."

"Those ones are gross," Jenny said. "You can have them."

"Emily ate all the grape," I said. "But she's gone next week, and I put fudgsicles on the grocery list, so we'll see what happens."

We heard the wail of a police siren, and everyone tensed. All the times Constable Postma or whoever had come to the pool, it had never been lights and siren. The sound was fading out fast. They were probably on the highway towards Seaforth, called away by who knows what. There were meth labs, but I couldn't imagine Jake Postma going into any of those. I didn't think of him as that kind of cop, even though he absolutely was. He tried to be everyone's big brother or favourite son in town, but that didn't change the badge.

Maybe he just really wanted fish and chips.

28.
Maddie Carter

In the end, it was very easy to start a fire.

The Chasers headed up to their cottage the second last week of August with no plans to return until after Labour Day Weekend. The Pedersens brought the beans in a week after that. It was a dry August, so the field was light brown and cracked. The furrows were deep and uneven, but not unmanageable. The birding club even took the week off, because they were so sick of wild turkeys that they were just going to go to the beach instead.

Jenny had the gas in her car. Louise had bought it a few days ago in Kincardine, after driving Paul up for a baseball game. The plan was that we would have a sleepover at Louise's house. Her parents were gone, Paul slept like a rock, and Aaron was finally living in the second house, since he'd managed to fix the electric and plumbing. Jenny would drive.

The night of the fire, we were all too excited to sleep. It was nominally Jenny's birthday party, so Louise had decorated and baked just like she usually would. I was too worked up to eat much, but at least I didn't get a sugar buzz. We watched movies, and Mags might have dozed a little, but finally it was two a.m., and time to go.

"There might be a thunderstorm," Jen whispered as we pulled on our shoes and headed for Jenny's car as stealthily as possible.

"Why are you whispering?" I asked at a normal volume.

"I don't know." Jen sounded disgruntled. "It felt like I should."

"Please don't make me more nervous than I am," Jenny said. "I still have to drive."

Louise had plotted the route carefully, drawing it on a paper map from the local tourist kiosk and then burning it at one of Mags's bonfire nights. It was by no means the direct way, but it was the quietest streets and the emptiest side roads. She even mapped out where Jenny would turn her lights off. On the way back, we wouldn't come through town at all.

We all piled into the car, Louise in the front because she was absolutely the most likely to keep a level head and give directions. I was squeezed between Mags and Jen in the back. Mags grabbed my hand, and even though it was almost completely dark, I could see the gleam in her eyes.

It's hard to explain darkness to someone who has only ever lived in cities or what passes for a small town on television. The Jantzis had barn lights and porch lights, but at this time of night, only the lone streetlight they had attached to the hydro pole was still on. The whole front yard was bathed in an orange glow that was much more customarily seen on pavement than it was on grass. We had spent hours playing under that light over the years. Louise's parents had installed it so the kids could play outside after dark, and we certainly had.

Jenny started the car and pulled slowly out of the driveway and onto the concession. Once she was facing away from Aaron's house, she turned the headlights on. She drove down to the paved side road that led into town and turned onto it. I'd been driving on these roads my whole life, but Louise sent us on so many twists and turns that I felt like I was lost about ten minutes in. Now there were no lights at all, only the occasional house or warning light on top of a silo. The glow of Eganston was in front of us, a beacon to orient us in the night.

It took ten more minutes to turn onto the Pedersens' concession. The Chaser house was totally dark, only a few security lights on the barn. The Pedersens had a row of trees along the side of their property. During the day, they were distinguished and interesting yard markers. At night, we could only see the odd spindly branch when it was in front of a light. Jenny put the car in park and turned off the headlights. She reached up and pressed the button that would stop the inside light from coming on when one of us opened a door.

We had decided that only two of us would go into the field. I had the gas container, and Mags had a BBQ starter, along with like four backups. We waited in the car, giving our eyes a while to get used to the dark. We had to do this and cause as little disturbance to the ground as we could, which meant we couldn't just go blundering through the ditch. After five agonizing minutes, Mags took a deep breath.

"Ready?" I asked, pulling on my gloves.

"Let's go," she said.

Jen kissed me on the forehead, and Mags and I slid out of the back seat. Jenny popped the trunk and then took Louise's hand. When we were moving, Louise was fine, but waiting was difficult for her nerves. I hefted the gas can, Mags checked the lighters for the fifteenth time, and we headed slowly down the bank.

There wasn't enough light for us to be able to read the billboard. Its hateful message was obscured. Amelia couldn't accidentally look out her bedroom window at night and see the message her ex's parents wanted to make sure she got. I wondered if she had curtains.

In the dark, the furrows seemed about a million times more uneven. Mags and I went slowly. It was almost pitch black and super quiet. We could hear cars on the highway two concessions over, but only one every few minutes. Once we heard the speed bumps on Mill Road. Those noises were always clearer at night. You could hear the speed bumps in town if it was quiet enough.

I unscrewed the lid on the gas can and carefully poured gas down one of the huge stakes that supported the billboard. It smelled strongly, but that was hardly a surprise. I took a few steps over to do the other one, and then placed the canister on the ground, where it would get caught in the blaze and melt. I threw my gloves down, too, and then went to stand with Mags. She had the lighter in her hand already, her finger on the button.

"This is insane," she said. "I regret absolutely nothing, but this is insane."

"The alternative *is* nothing," I reminded her. "We want them to know we don't approve."

Originally, we had discussed setting the fire just before a thunderstorm in the hope that it would be dismissed as a lightning strike. The timing was too awkward and there were too many factors left to chance, but to be completely honest, I wanted people to know it wasn't an accident. I wanted them to know, beyond a shadow of a doubt, that someone did this because they believed the billboard was cruel and wrong.

It was going to take the fire department about ten minutes to get out here. They were volunteers, so they all had to assemble at the station before they could go anywhere. We'd all been through the fire hall a bunch of times when we were in Brownies, and most recently on Canada Day, when they had hosted breakfast. It had been incredibly easy to get Teddy to ask them questions about how the fire station worked.

"Well," said Mags, "I guess I should do this before Louise eats her own liver. Do you want to?"

It was a nice offer, but this was as much hers as it was mine. She still thought of herself as Catholic, but it was a tenuous hold at best. I knew she wanted to do it as much as I wanted it done.

"No," I told her. "It's all yours."

The first stake went up immediately, flames racing along the streams of gasoline that were running down the wood from where I'd poured. Mags didn't stop to watch the fire. She was already moving to the second stake. It went up just as easily, and she tossed her gloves into the flames. We knew from crime shows that most arsonists get caught because they hang around to watch, either the fire or the response. We didn't care about either of those things, so we were up the ditch before the bottom of the billboard caught, and back in the car before the fire was bright enough to see from any distance.

Jenny put the car in drive, and we headed off on Louise's route. The impulse to press the pedal and fly must have been excruciating. I was in the back seat, and I could hardly stand how slow we were going. But Jenny's hands were firm on the steering wheel as she drove farther away from town, and her speed was steady. Louise was narrating the turns, and we were halfway to Londesborough before we started hearing sirens far behind us.

29.

Maddie Carter

After twenty minutes of seemingly random turns in the dark of the countryside, Louise started navigating us back towards her house. We weren't going through town at all, but we would have to drive along the main highway for a couple of kilometres between gravel roads. The trees that lined the side road we were on now were thick, and so we didn't see the flashing police lights until after we turned onto the paved road.

"They've seen us," Louise said. "You have to keep going."

"I'm going to have to talk to them!" Jenny said. "It's a traffic stop!"

"It's okay," Jen said. "You can do this. Just tell them you're out for a drive with friends."

"It's almost three in the morning!" Jenny said. Somehow she was still driving steadily, but I was starting to panic. If we got caught, it would be my fault. This was my wish.

"We're heading into town from a completely different direction," Mags said. "There's no reason for them to be suspicious."

"And they wouldn't suspect us anyway," I said, finally finding my voice. "Remember why we are the ones who are doing this."

Jenny squared her shoulders, her hands a perfect ten and two on the wheel, and braked for the silhouetted police officer who was waving her down. She put the window down, and I heard Mags breathe a sigh of relief. It was Constable Postma.

"Jenny?" he said. Clearly he had not been expecting a car full of teenagers.

"Hi, Jake," Jenny said. "I mean Constable Postma . . . Officer?"

I couldn't tell if she was nervous or acting nervous, but she was perfect.

"What are you girls doing out here?" Constable Postma asked. "It's so late."

"Oh," said Jenny, turning on the customer service voice that had got her through all those years at the grocery store without murdering someone. "Well, it's silly, but you know, we're all leaving soon. It's my birthday and we were hanging out at Louise's, and we couldn't sleep, and we just wanted to, you know, go out one more time."

The constable leaned on the window, looking at us in the back seat. He didn't flash his light in our faces at least.

"I totally understand," he said. "I came back, but the magic's never quite the same."

He tapped the roof of the car.

"Look, I know none of you were drinking, but there was an incident outside of town tonight, and I'm supposed to encourage people to stay off the roads for the emergency vehicles." He sounded so earnest I almost laughed.

"Oh my gosh, is everyone okay?" Louise asked, leaning forwards so that Constable Postma could see her.

"Yeah, as far as I know," he said. "Just some property damage. But it would be best if you girls headed back to the Jantzis', okay?"

"Yes, sir," Jenny said. "We were headed that way anyway. Can we drive past you or do you want us to double back?"

He looked up and down the dark and empty road. I couldn't see his face, even in the flashing lights, but I imagined he was wishing he had a better assignment than babysitting a mostly deserted traffic stop.

"Go ahead," he said. "Just remember to drive carefully, and go straight home."

"We will!" Jenny said.

He stepped away, and she rolled up the window before easing down on the gas and pulling away from him. None of us made any noise at all as we drove. I was holding my breath, and I think everyone else might have been, too. There was complete silence until we turned onto Louise's concession.

"Holy shit," Jen said, the words bursting out of her chest.

"No one is allowed to lose their minds until I have put the car in park," Jenny said. "Hold it together for like three more minutes."

We managed, but as soon as the car stopped moving, it was like a wave of hysteria breaking through us. Louise finally put her head on the dashboard and breathed hard, but Jenny basically rolled out of the car and lay down on the grass in the front yard. Jen opened the door, and we all slid out behind her. I heard Louise moving, and before long, all five of us were lying on the ground. It was wet and cool, but not too uncomfortable. Above us, the stars were bright.

"Jenny, you were amazing," I said.

"I thought I was going to vomit," she admitted. "Though I guess that might have worked, too, in terms of getting rid of him."

"It was perfect," Mags said. "We were all perfect."

"I didn't even do anything," Jen pointed out.

"Sure you did," I told her. "You were here. We were all here."

We stayed down for a few more minutes, and then all of the adrenaline seemed to run out of us at the same time.

"I'm exhausted," I said. "Let's go back upstairs."

We heaved ourselves up and crossed the yard, and then climbed the ladder back to the rumpus room. The beginning and the end. Where the wishes had started, and where we'd made big decisions.

"Come on," Mags said. "We have to wash our hands for like an hour."

I followed her into the bathroom and pulled a piece of hair to my nose to smell it for smoke. That would be harder to wash out.

"That's why we roasted marshmallows, remember," Mags reminded me.

"Oh, right," I said. We all smelled like smoke because we'd had a bonfire. It had been a last-minute addition to the plan, but it was a good one.

I went back into the rumpus room to find everyone sitting on their sleeping bags waiting for us. Mags was right behind me. The girls were looking at me, like they expected I'd have something deep and meaningful to say. Something about how we'd changed in the last year, or how this would make us stronger going forwards, but to be perfectly honest, even though I was tired, I could only think of one thing.

"Louise," I said. "I'm starving. Can we get the cake?"

A LETTER TO THE EDITOR

We said we were never going to tell anyone. And we haven't.

The undeniable part is this: the transgressions, the abuses of power, the pretended ignorance, the flat-out refusal to see pain in another person.

There has been too much whispering in the world of girls. You haven't protected us. You stopped trying the moment we became slightly inconvenient. You let us get hurt. Your hurt us yourselves. It is time to breathe fire. It is time to scream.

You won't know who we were.

You won't know how many of us took part.

You won't even be exactly sure what we did.

You will never suspect us.

But you'll always wonder. Not why we did it, but how.

After all, you made us.

And we won't let you ignore that—or anyone—anymore.

Sincerely,
The Good Girls

ACKNOWLEDGMENTS

I just want you all to know that nothing in this book actually happened. Except for all the parts that did.

Thank you, as always, to Andrew, who received a list with about fifteen books on it and picked the one I knew he would. It was a hard call, but it was the right one.

Thanks also to Josh, and everyone at Adams Literary, for helping me manage my writing schedule, and for making sure I had a writing schedule to manage.

Team Penguin, you're awesome. Thank you especially to cover designers Maria Fazio and Theresa Evangelista for being extremely patient while I learned to talk about graphic design and we all realized that EVERYTHING was going to be post-Barbie pink if we weren't careful.

I'd be stuck forever without the Broken Home, the Trifecta, Leanne Van Loo, Dahlia Adler, Joanne Levy, Ashley Eckstein, and various experts that I was lucky enough to consult.

And finally, thank you to the readers who followed me back to the E. K. Johnston Multiverse for the first time since 2017.